DEAD

INSIDE

(A Kelsey Hawk Mystery—Book 1)

Kate Bold

Kate Bold

Bestselling author Kate Bold is author of the ALEXA CHASE SUSPENSE THRILLER series, comprising six books (and counting); the ASHLEY HOPE SUSPENSE THRILLER series, comprising six books (and counting); the CAMILLE GRACE FBI SUSPENSE THRILLER series, comprising eight books (and counting); the HARLEY COLE FBI SUSPENSE THRILLER series, comprising eleven books (and counting); the KAYLIE BROOKS PSYCHOLOGICAL SUSPENSE THRILLER series, comprising five books (and counting); the EVE HOPE FBI SUSPENSE THRILLER series, comprising seven books (and counting); the DYLAN FIRST FBI SUSPENSE THRILLER series, comprising five books (and counting); the LAUREN LAMB FBI SUSPENSE THRILLER series, comprising five books (and counting); and the KELSEY HAWK MYSTERY series, comprising five books (and counting).

An avid reader and lifelong fan of the mystery and thriller genres, Kate loves to hear from you, so please feel free to visit www.kateboldauthor.com to learn more and stay in touch.

BOOKS BY KATE BOLD

KELSEY HAWK MYSTERY
DEAD INSIDE (Book #1)
DEAD RECKONING (Book #2)
DEAD TO ME (Book #3)
DEAD SILENCE (Book #4)
DEAD TO DAWN (Book #5)

ALEXA CHASE SUSPENSE THRILLER
THE KILLING GAME (Book #1)
THE KILLING TIDE (Book #2)
THE KILLING HOUR (Book #3)
THE KILLING POINT (Book #4)
THE KILLING FOG (Book #5)
THE KILLING PLACE (Book #6)

ASHLEY HOPE SUSPENSE THRILLER
LET ME GO (Book #1)
LET ME OUT (Book #2)
LET ME LIVE (Book #3)
LET ME BREATHE (Book #4)
LET ME FORGET (Book #5)
LET ME ESCAPE (Book #6)

CAMILLE GRACE FBI SUSPENSE THRILLER
NOT ME (Book #1)
NOT NOW (Book #2)
NOT WELL (Book #3)
NOT HER (Book #4)
NOT NORMAL (Book #5)
NOT AGAIN (Book #6)
NOT SAFE (Book #7)
NOT TODAY (Book #8)

HARLEY COLE FBI SUSPENSE THRILLER
NOWHERE SAFE (Book #1)
NOWHERE LEFT (Book #2)

NOWHERE TO RUN (Book #3)
NOWHERE LIKE THIS (Book #4)
NOWHERE GIRL (Book #5)
NOWHERE TO HIDE (Book #6)
NOWHERE CERTAIN (Book #7)
NOWHERE PURE (Book #8)
NOWHERE SOUND (Book #9)
NOWHERE SANE (Book #10)
NOWHERE TRUE (Book #11)

KAYLIE BROOKS PYSCHOLOGICAL SUSPENSE THRILLER
LAST BREATH (Book #1)
LAST CHANCE (Book #2)
LAST WISH (Book #3)
LAST SHOT (Book #4)
LAST MISTAKE (Book #5)

EVE HOPE FBI SUSPENSE THRILLER
IN HIS BLOOD (Book #1)
IN HIS SIGHTS (Book #2)
IN HIS REACH (Book #3)
IN HIS MIND (Book #4)
IN HIS WAY (Book #5)
IN HIS THOUGHTS (Book #6)
IN HIS DREAMS (Book #7)

DYLAN FIRST FBI SUSPENSE THRILLER
OUT OF REACH (Book #1)
OUT OF TOUCH (Book #2)
OUT OF TIME (Book #3)
OUT OF BOUNDS (Book #4)
OUT OF LUCK (Book #5)

LAUREN LAMB FBI SUSPENSE THRILLER
SOMETHING KNOCKING (Book #1)
SOMETHING CALLING (Book #2)
SOMETHING WRONG (Book 3)
SOMETHING DARK (Book #4)
SOMETHING TO HIDE (Book #5)

PROLOGUE

The shrill scream brought John Gallant out of his trance—a blood-curdling scream that could only mean death.

He had been staring out into space, half-watching his daughter, Kimberly, as she waved at him from the small tea cup that was going round and round in front of him. The afternoon had become chilly, and even though he had told her to keep her jacket on, she was waving it around like a rodeo cowboy. The whole ride had a mesmerizing effect on him, and it had taken only a few minutes for him to lose all focus and stare at the colored tea cups swishing around in front of him.

The scream quickly shattered all that, and he instinctively ducked and turned to where it was coming from. In the distance, a crowd of people had begun to run in various directions, and soon enough, the first scream was joined by a second and a third.

John shuddered. He had heard that scream before, back during his tour in Iraq, when his recon mission had been ambushed and the casualties included soldiers and civilians alike. It was the kind of scream that pierced through the air and somehow found its way inside him, grabbing every nerve fiber and tugging until he could feel his head explode.

"Daddy!"

Kimberly's voice barely registered amid the chaos that had begun to overcome the North Dakota Winter Fair, and it took him a minute to calm his senses and let his body switch to autopilot. He glanced toward the stage to see the cause of the terror—in the midst of the light-hearted ice sculptures was a woman frozen in time. She was more than frozen in time; she was frozen in ice.

Quickly, he jumped the small fence that separated the spectators from the riders and snatched Kimberly from the moving cup as it slowed to a stop. Grabbing her hand, he quickly led her out and towards where his wife was waiting.

Samantha Gallant was already running to them. "What the hell is going on?" she yelled, frantic fear in her eyes as they darted around, taking in the stampede of festival visitors running towards the exits.

1

"Take Kim to the car and wait for me there," John shouted over the commotion. "If I'm not out in twenty minutes, drive home."

"John!" Samantha shouted after him as he raced away. "John!"

John ignored her and picked up the pace, weaving between the crowds running against him. He pulled out his Glock and badge, making sure they were visible, and scanned the crowd, trying to make sense of what everyone was fleeing from. In the distance, a dozen or so yards away, the festival security was surrounding the ice sculpture display stage, and a tarp was being pulled over one of them.

Moving to the flank of the crowd, he rushed towards the stage, his eyes darting back and forth as he studied the crowd for anything out of place. By the time he reached the displays, two security guards had made their way to intercept him.

"Move!" John yelled, holding his badge, and rushing past them before they could register what was happening. "Keep everyone back!"

Jumping on the stage, he slowed down and took in the stage master's expression. Dread, fear, terror...any of those could describe the man's look. His hands held the tarp tight, bright white at the knuckles, and he shook like a leaf.

John put a hand on the man's shoulder, startling him. "What's going on?" John asked.

"I put the tarp back on as quickly as I could, but...." The stage master let go of the tarp and shook his head, taking a few steps back before dropping to his knees. John grabbed the tarp and pulled it aside. He dropped it immediately, taking a few involuntary steps back when he saw the display beneath.

Enclosed in the single, large block of bloody ice, a woman stared at him with dead eyes and a frozen scream.

CHAPTER ONE

"Screw this!"

She knew she should wait for backup. She knew this was the type of behavior her boss would use to get rid of her once and for all. You can't have a small-town girl besting everyone else in the big-city precinct, after all. And she knew she was putting her own life in danger.

She knew many things, but knowledge didn't matter when a child was in danger.

Kelsey Hawk loved her job, but she cared more about what the job actually entailed—serving and protecting. Protocols didn't protect, and bureaucracy didn't serve. She pulled her 40 caliber pistol from its holster, crouched, and made her way toward the run-down ranch house across the field.

"If I get fired for this, then so be it," she muttered.

Keeping to the tree line, hoping the shadows cast by the setting sun would hide her, she moved with expert precision toward the east side of the house, her eyes never leaving the front door.

It had taken her three months to find the bastard, and she would not let protocol stop her from finally bringing him in.

A small shed gave her a few seconds of shelter, and she took the time to scan the house from a closer vantage point. The paint was peeling off in numerous areas, and the roof needed a lot of work. The patio showed signs of a termite infestation, but the one thing that stood out was the newly installed windows. From where she sat, they looked double-layered, meant to keep noise out.

Or keep noise in.

Three months.

She had been assigned to missing persons less than a year ago, and it had taken a lot of legwork and long nights to finally figure out the logistics of how the Carlone family was smuggling its victims into and out of New Jersey. Kelsey had been able to narrow it down to one man, Oscar Solasky, a small-town black market smuggler who had moved up into what he considered "merchandise," and she was certain she could have found him faster if not for the red tape slowing her down.

She cursed the FBI when it came to acting fast.

A shadow moved swiftly across the window, and Kelsey hid behind the shed. Taking a few deep breaths, she looked back the way she had come. There were no flashing lights, no certainty that her warrant was on its way, accompanied by the SWAT team she needed to get Oscar into custody.

It's all down to you, Kels.

Kelsey closed her eyes tight, trying to forget the pictures she had been shown. It was horrific to look at pictures of dead bodies, victims, but nothing prepared you for those who were taken and kept alive for... *fun*. The images would haunt her until the end of her days.

Files, interviews, statements, CCTV footage, DNA evidence, gossip, circumstantial evidence—it all ran rapidly through her head like she was flicking through microfilm slides. It built the case in her mind; they only needed to get him—Oscar. Yet, that wasn't her focus. All she could think about was his method of working. The FBI's red tape made them slow, too slow on one previous occasion to stop him from...

No, not this time! No matter what happens to me.

Kelsey counted back from ten, waiting for the adrenaline to kick in. Once she was sure she was ready, she gave the horizon another look— she was on her own. If she waited any longer, she would miss her window of opportunity.

Kelsey gave the house one final sweep before breaking from her hiding spot and rushing toward the back at a low crouch. Once she reached the east wall, she pressed her back against it and slid towards the window. She didn't expect it to be open, but it gave her a pretty good view of what was inside.

A woman was tied up, gagged, and lay in a fetal position in a corner of the room. An open door revealed a second spacious room with a table, and a man sat with his back to her. The thinning hair and tattoo across his nape were all Kelsey needed to confirm her suspect. Oscar had no idea what was coming.

Sliding towards the back, she kept her ears open for the sounds of anyone else. She had scouted the house for a good hour, waiting for backup after she had called in her location. It was obvious no one was coming, or if they were, they were taking their sweet time. She often wondered if the Carlones had someone on the inside stalling things.

If they did, then Oscar would be gone already.

That didn't change the fact that it was still a possibility, and the chance someone might still warn her suspect made Kelsey even edgier. She had to move fast.

Carefully climbing up the back patio, bracing herself for the creaks that might give her away, she edged toward the back door, almost shaking with fear. She had not felt this way before, but she had also not come this close to a psychopath. A thin barrier of wood separated her from the face of evil—to read about him was one thing; to face him was quite another. Kelsey took one final breath—time was not on her side.

Her hand was barely on the knob when the door flew open, and a body slammed into her, taking her by surprise and knocking the wind out of her. She fell to the ground hard, the heavy weight of her attacker still on top of her, fists slamming into the side of her head. She was back in Mikkisula, Missouri, again, only nine years old, and Rachel Barlow stood over her laughing. Rachel had punched her repeatedly until Kelsey had the good sense to lie down and not get back up. The humiliation and fear caught in her throat, but she didn't cry; she stifled the tears, holding them back. She would not lie down and take what others gave anymore.

The world around her swam, and on instinct, she lifted her knee to throw the man off her. There was no humiliation here, only pure terror.

A loud holler of pain followed the attack, and she could feel her knee connect with the soft tissue of the man's groin. His weight fell off her, and she quickly jumped to her feet and lunged at him. She reached for the gun on her hip, but she hadn't seen him grab a branch. It connected with her wrist—there was no crack or snap, but there was a bright flash of pain. She fumbled the gun and dropped it to the ground. Another swing of the branch, and she brought her injured arm up to block it. This time there *was* a crack as the dry branch splintered in two.

Raw determination replaced the pain in her arm as she lunged forward again, surprising Oscar. He swung at her with a meaty fist, but she was too close, and the inside of his arm caught her dully on the temple. Kelsey brought her knee up again, a tactic that had worked so well the first time that it deserved a second shot, and as soon as he bent forward a little, she slammed the palm of her hand into his nose. Another crack—an intensely satisfying one.

Oscar glared at her, blood streaming from his nose, red fire in his eyes. He had meant to murder the young girl in the house, and the look

5

in his eyes told Kelsey he would happily add another to the menu. He took a confident step forward, unaware of the half-branch in Kelsey's hand.

She stood tall to face him, and as soon as he moved to strike her again, she brought it up to his chin, snapping his head backward and snapping away her fear of the man. Oscar tumbled backward. Kelsey was too well-trained to stop now. She fell on him. He didn't have it in him to fight back, and in a quick motion, she had Oscar Solasky pinned to the ground with his arm around his back.

"Oscar Solasky," Kelsey breathed, the ringing in her ears intensifying, "you are under arrest. You have the right to remain silent."

As she continued through the man's rights, Oscar tried to wiggle out from under her, and she pressed a knee against his shoulder, forcing another holler of pain out of him. She cuffed him, pulled him to his feet, and pushed him towards the house.

"You have no idea what you're doing!" he screamed at her. "You're going to die for this! Your whole family is going to burn!"

Kelsey sighed, her relief flowing freely. "My whole family's already dead," she breathed, slamming him into the door frame on their way in, the sound of bones breaking making her smile slightly. He could do nothing to hurt her.

"My nose!" Oscar screamed.

"Sorry," Kelsey replied, "just wanted to make sure."

She forced him into the room where the woman lay and threw him into a corner. One look at his whimpering face assured her he wouldn't be trying anything stupid. Kelsey held the gun in one hand and used the other to untie the terrified woman bound on the floor.

More trauma. Kelsey had been through trauma, and now this woman had too. Her only hope was that the woman would not become as messed up as she was.

"What's your name?" Kelsey asked.

"M-Maria." She looked up at Kelsey, holding her gaze, not daring to look elsewhere. She was around thirty years old, but the ordeal had turned her into a meek, little girl. Kelsey wanted to embrace her and tell her everything was going to be all right, but experience held her back.

"My name is Kelsey, and I'm going to take care of you. Everything is going to be fine." Kelsey could see her own fear reflected in the woman's eyes. She had almost died coming in here, and she had no doubt she would be reamed out for it, but that was not the root of the fear. She had saved a life, but it didn't change anything about her past. It didn't remove the shame or guilt.

Kelsey helped the woman to sit up against the wall and slumped beside her, pointing the gun at Oscar, his shirt stained red. He didn't take his eyes off Kelsey or the woman.

Two minutes later, the FBI finally arrived with a cacophony of sirens, followed by a chorus of shouts and drum-beat footsteps.

Kelsey held in the tears that threatened to roll down her cheeks. The FBI agents looked at her with frustration as they entered and cleaned things up as if she had made their jobs harder by saving someone.

Always one step behind and five minutes too late! If I had waited any longer, he would have thrown her into the back of his truck, and we would never have seen her again.

Alexander strode through the house, his footsteps slow and deliberate. He shook his head and handed her a radio. One of the female agents helped the woman to her feet—Maria fixed her eyes on Kelsey—her savior—but she was eventually pried away.

Alexander nodded silently, approving of what she had done. Before he turned, he mouthed, "Granger."

Kelsey steeled herself and pressed the button on the side. "Sir, we found her. I just want to—" She was cut off before explaining why she had disregarded a direct order and gone in alone.

"My office! NOW!" Granger demanded.

CHAPTER TWO

"Hey, Hawk? How many strikes do you get before you are out?" Special Agent Bobby Carter asked.

Kelsey had stopped at her desk, hoping to find some solace there—an answer to all her problems--but they were piled up in her mind like the paperwork on her desk. She would get to it someday. She looked from Bobby to the stacks of files, though someday might never come now that she had gone ahead and saved a young girl in the *wrong* way.

"Three strikes is usually how the game is played, but when your boss is umpire, pitcher, and... do you know what, Carter? I don't have time for this. I might as well get this over with now and move on with my life."

She wanted to say her boss was the rule maker of the game too. Sure, she had been pig-headed and gone in ahead of everyone else, but she had saved that young woman, and that was a win in anyone's book.

Not in Paul Granger's book, her Special Agent in Charge. He had been looking for a way to get rid of her since she was moved to his field office. She was too young, eager, and good at her job. She made the other recruits nervous, and that made Paul Granger nervous.

He was good at his job—there was no doubt about it—but he was used to special agents following his orders exactly and not in creative ways.

Kelsey headed to the bathroom first. She placed her hands down on the surface around the sink and stared into the mirror, shaking her head. She could blame her SAC all she wanted, but she only had herself to blame.

The toilet flushed, and Special Agent Amanda Briggins emerged from the cubicle. She jumped and placed a hand on her chest.

"I didn't hear you come in," she said, chuckling.

"You need to work on your perception and awareness to get ahead, Mandy," Kelsey smiled.

"It's not going to be the same around here if you…."

Kelsey frowned. "I'm not gone yet." She pushed a lock of black hair behind her ear. "You have me around for at least another ten minutes if I draw this out."

Amanda washed her hands, glancing up occasionally to look at Kelsey.

Kelsey wanted to lay it all out on the table and tell her acquaintance (did she consider Amanda her friend?) that she had fought her entire life to keep up and get ahead, which had gotten her into trouble. Kelsey needed to be the best, but only because being as good was not good enough for a woman in the FBI. She had to stick her neck out and stay ahead, but when the executioner held the axe above her, sticking her neck out was not always the best option.

Amanda patted Kelsey's back before leaving the washroom.

Kelsey pushed up the skin on her forehead—it was still tight and supple, as it should be for someone only just touching her mid-twenties, but Kelsey was sure small creases were appearing. The stress of the job, and she was only nine months out of Quantico.

She took a deep breath and turned to face the music. When she exited the bathroom, it felt like all eyes were on her. She made the long walk to Paul Granger's office and lifted her hand to knock on the glass door.

"Get your ass in here, Hawk!" SAC Granger called.

Kelsey took a deep breath and pushed the door open—she ventured into the fray.

"Sit down!" Granger shouted before the door closed.

She did as she was told, remaining silent. She wanted to plead her case, but that had only made things worse the first two times she had been called into her SAC's office to be reamed out. It was best to stay quiet—and when he told her she was being fired, she would plead her case without fear of repercussions.

"What were you thinking?" Granger stood with his back to her, facing the window overlooking the city. He didn't even do her the courtesy of turning around to face her.

I mean nothing to you!

"How's the victim?" Kelsey asked plainly.

The question irritated Granger, going by the tension in his shoulders, and it finally got him to turn around.

"Zero agents," Granger stated. "That is the number of agents I have lost on active duty. Do you know when I will allow myself to lose an agent in the field?"

9

Kelsey knew better than to answer that question.

"Never," he finished. "I have not lost an agent, and I will not lose an agent, Hawk. Not even you."

Not even me! It would dent your fragile ego, wouldn't it? You wouldn't mourn me, only your perfect record.

"Is Oscar Solasky in custody, sir?" Kelsey asked.

She had to remain professional—it was the only thing that gave her the upper hand. And she knew it pained him that she had been the one to save the woman, that she had been the one to subdue Solasky.

Again, he ignored her. "A ship can't sail straight and true without the crew following the orders of its captain, Hawk. What makes you so different from everyone else?"

The ship metaphor again—Kelsey had heard it half a dozen times. She didn't know what made her different from everyone else. She needed to prove herself and get ahead of the competition. Yet, she had followed the careers of multiple female FBI agents, most of whom had followed the rules and gotten ahead. What made her so special?

SAC Granger let out an end-of-the-road sigh. "It makes my job much easier, Hawk. It's all been signed off by the director. Today's your last day here."

Kelsey expected it, but it still hit like a bullet to the chest. "You don't need to wish me—"

"Monday will be your first day in the Winchburgh field office," Granger interrupted.

"Winchburgh?" Kelsey racked her brain; she had heard that name before.

Granger smiled. "Nice little outpost in North Dakota."

That's where she knew it from—she had read a case file from that field office when she was training at Quantico. It was the biggest case to have ever happened in the area. Three people and one cow had been killed. She knew why her SAC was smiling so wide.

"You start there Monday," Granger reminded.

People often use the phrase, *a fate worse than death*. Well, a posting in North Dakota was a fate worse than being fired for Kelsey. She might have quit on the spot if she did not love the job so much. And she was damn good at it, no matter what her superiors thought.

"Thank you, sir," Kelsey mustered. She did all she could to hide her anger and frustration.

The smile on Granger's face remained as he flicked his hand to dismiss Kelsey.

Special Agent Kelsey Hawk removed herself from her SAC's office. Joining the FBI was her ticket out of the Midwest. She had gone from small-town girl to big-city special agent. Now, Kelsey was right back where she started—no, it was two steps back down the ladder. A small town. Long, cold winters. A place where nothing ever happened.

A place where she had nowhere to go—no rise to greatness, nowhere to fall, only consistent mediocrity.

The only thing left was to convince her fiancé he should move to Winchburgh with her—and they could be miserable in small-town North Dakota together.

***

"Hey, you would not believe the day I have had." Kelsey tossed her bag onto the hook just inside the door and started kicking off her shoes. "I don't know how to say this, but—"

Kelsey stopped and placed a hand on her hip; her gun was stored securely at her field office. Kelsey did not have to put her FBI-issued observation skills to good use to know someone was in her home—someone who should not be there.

She relaxed as much as her body let her when she heard the music coming from the living room. Still, she wished she had a weapon of some sort; she was in no mood for anything or anyone. Kelsey crept closer to the living room door and pressed her ear to it. All she could hear was the music, but slightly louder.

Kelsey thought about turning around and getting the hell out of there, but she had already burst into one crime scene by herself, so why not another? A lump rose in her throat as she lay her hand on the handle. She turned it and swung the door open inward.

Darren jumped up from the couch imminently at the interruption, so hastily that he almost spilled the glass of wine in his hand. He was flustered but quickly regained his composure. It took all Kelsey had not to launch herself at Darren or the woman he was sharing a bottle of wine with.

"What are you doing here?" he asked.

Kelsey frowned. "What am I doing here? You mean in my own home? What are you *doing* here, Darren?"

"You weren't supposed to be home until late. I thought you had that big case."

"Should I call ahead?" Kelsey asked. "If I'm considering coming home early, should I call ahead, Darren? Huh? Should I call ahead just in case you are *doing* something?"

"Come on! Don't be like that, Kels! You remember Belinda from work, don't you?"

Kelsey folded her arms. "I certainly won't forget her in a hurry."

Belinda remained pinned to the couch like a mouse trying to remain invisible while two cats prowled the room.

"Can you please... not!" Darren said. He looked over at Belinda. "Belinda came around to review some reports, and she's having a hard time at work, so I comforted her. I'm a shoulder to cry on, Kels. Is that a crime nowadays?"

Where is my shoulder to cry on? I'm supposed to get on with it because I chose the job and knew the nature of it beforehand.

"Do you really think I am an idiot, Darren?" Kelsey demanded. "Do you really think I would believe this shit? At least do it somewhere a little more private and not our house!"

Belinda squirmed on the couch and finally rose. "I should, um, go." She put the glass down on the coffee table.

"Don't forget your reports, Belinda," Kelsey goaded.

"What?" Belinda looked lost again.

"I'll bring them to work on Monday," Darren said. "Don't worry about any of this, all right?"

Kelsey waved her hands in the air. "Yeah, don't worry about any of this, *Belinda.*"

She hated how riled up she was. Kelsey had a good reason to be riled up, but she had managed to subdue a child trafficker, save a woman from being killed, and then be reamed out by her boss without losing her cool. Yet, she couldn't keep her composure now. And because of what? Her marriage was over before it had even begun.

Kelsey turned away and wiped her eyes with the back of her hand. She would not give either of them the satisfaction of seeing her cry. She should have been hysterical and broken down just like her life was breaking down, but she was an FBI special agent, and her professionalism kicked in.

The front door closed behind Belinda.

"Well, thank you for that," Darren sighed. He collected Belinda's glass from the coffee table and took it with his own to the kitchen.

Kelsey shook her head and followed him. "I want to look over the numbers too."

"What?" Darren dumped the wine down the sink and rinsed the glasses.

"I got an early finish today, and I want to help you, Darren. Let me take a look at the reports and see if I can help in any way."

"Jesus Christ, Kels!" Darren turned around to face her. "You're making a fool of yourself."

Kelsey looked back toward the living room. "I didn't see them back there. Did you file them away before being a shoulder to cry on?"

"Is it because I was comforting her? Is that it? I would do that for you, Kels, if you let me. But, no! You have to be strong and independent! It's not a weakness to ask for help," Darren shouted.

Kelsey hated that he was right. She didn't like to show weakness in any way, and his behavior with Belinda made her feel weak. She was young and attractive with a good job, but it was not enough to satisfy her fiancé. That only meant she was lacking elsewhere. Maybe she was a bad person, boring, controlling.

She shook her head again, but this time to remove the thoughts. He was the one in the wrong, not her. They could have avoided this if he had only spoken to her about his feelings.

"She was practically sitting in your lap," Kelsey said sadly. "Am I not good enough for you?"

"Hey, don't say that, babe." Darren closed in on her and placed a hand on her cheek.

Kelsey wanted to pull away, but after her day, the intimacy was welcome.

"I love you, Kels," Darren said.

"I know you do," Kelsey admitted, "and I love you too, but what good is that anymore? At least be a man and admit that you fucked up!"

Darren's hand was instantly removed from Kelsey's cheek. His eyebrow twitched slightly, but he also held in his anger and frustration. He held her gaze for a full ten seconds.

"What do you expect, Kelsey?" The intonation in his voice sent a chill down Kelsey's spine. "You work eighty hours a week, and then you're too tired for anything when you get home. What am I supposed to do?"

"You are supposed to talk to me instead of jumping into bed with your secretary. I mean, how cliché can you get, Darren?"

"It didn't mean anything," Darren claimed.

"We both know this is not the first time or the first girl," Kelsey said.

"How do you know about that?"

Kelsey scoffed. "I didn't until right now. I'm leaving for North Dakota on Monday."

"What?" Darren furrowed his brow. "Listen, we can work this out. You don't have to go to your mother's."

Kelsey scoffed again and headed for the stairs to start packing. "You really are an asshole. I'm from Missouri, not North Dakota—you know nothing about me, do you?"

Darren followed her to the stairs. "Well, forgive me for forgetting one simple detail while our entire relationship collapses around us."

Kelsey climbed to the landing and turned around to look down on Darren at the bottom of the carpeted stairs. "It has collapsed, hasn't it?"

"I'll come with you," Darren claimed. "I'll take some time off, and we can vacation in North Dakota. Whatever you want, Kels."

"I wanted a husband, Darren—someone who would support and champion me. I know I can be hard to deal with sometimes, but this is messed up. How about I go to North Dakota on Monday, and you discuss your reports with Belinda? Maybe then, we can both be happy."

Darren was silent again, and it was all the confirmation Kelsey needed. She turned and walked up the rest of the stairs. She was walking away from the argument and Darren and her life here. It was a clean break, but the worst clean break imaginable.

Her relationship with her fiancé was over, and she had been sent off to Winchburgh to be buried amid cases that no one cared about.

Kelsey would be traveling somewhere else, but in reality she was going nowhere.

CHAPTER THREE

Kelsey expected the snow, but she still wasn't prepared for it. It was beautiful, majestic, and glorious, but it was a nightmare, too—a blanket of white that suffocated the small town of Winchburgh.

A fish out of water? Is that what I am? Maybe a shark in a small pond would be a more apt description.

Whichever way she thought about it, it was going to take a lot of adjusting. She had left Valleyview, a city with a larger population than the entire state of North Dakota, hating her life, but she arrived in the small town of Winchburgh (*population: 5443*) with renewed purpose. People had tried to hold her down her entire life, but she always found a way to resurface.

The town's population was written on the entrance, just like it had been in her small town back in Missouri. She never understood why it was a necessity.

Do they have to change it every time they have a birth or death? Or whenever someone leaves this godforsaken place?

The cry of a police car broke the monotony. Kelsey stopped at the almost deserted intersection in the middle of the town, checking her GPS again. A police car shot past at right angles, and it was followed soon after by another, the siren's tone changing in pitch to a long wail. A few seconds later, an ambulance and fire truck sped by.

That feels ominous. Maybe someone had a cow stolen.

When the light changed, Kelsey pressed on the gas and headed towards the FBI satellite office she had been told almost nothing about. Winter decorations hung from nearly every streetlight and business in the area, and her keen detective skills told her they were for the *Winter Fair*—keen detective skills and the fact that there were signs for it almost every five meters.

The office roof was covered in snow, and large snow banks sat in the parking lot. Kelsey was glad the parking spots had been cleared of snow—she had never driven on snow and did not want to start until she had settled in. So far, the roads had been clear.

15

Kelsey entered and found a man sitting at one of the two desks in the office. He must have been early thirties and was handsome enough in a small-town kind of way. He held himself with confidence and had an air of authority.

"Sir," Kelsey announced.

"Sir?" he replied.

"Are you my new SAC?" Kelsey looked around, hoping there was at least an internet connection.

"Sack?" he asked. "Sack of what?"

"It stands for Special Agent in Charge, and I am now just realizing that you are not."

The man stood up and extended a hand. "Deputy Sheriff John Gallant."

"Special Agent Kelsey Hawk." Kelsey took his hand and shook it. He had a firm grip, and she made sure to respond with a firm grip of her own.

"Looks like you brought your big-city crime with you," John noted.

"What do you mean?"

"Ah, we'll get to that," he clarified. "She's not going anywhere anytime soon. Might as well show you around first."

Kelsey couldn't help but think it had something to do with the four emergency vehicles she had seen on the way through town.

Maybe there's more here than meets the eye.

"All right, I'm your official welcoming party. Even with everything going on, I get to babysit you this morning." John held his hands up. "No offense meant; I know you outrank me, but things work differently here, so pay attention, or you will start off on the wrong foot. Sack? That's the boss, right? You'll be reporting to the Bismarck office. Special Agent Trevor Wood shares this office in Winchburgh, or he would, but he's out in Bismarck on a case for the foreseeable future, so you're the only one here for now. Lucky for us, the position was filled as quickly as it was."

John switched on one of the monitors. "I presume your company-issued passwords and whatnot will work here, and then you'll have access to whatever it is you need to gain access to."

Kelsey wasn't sure if he was annoyed with her or having to babysit her, not that she needed babysitting. If this was the grand tour of her office, it was quick and to the point. His bedside manner was lacking, but then, so was hers.

"I'll figure it all out," Kelsey said. She was happy to get through this quickly to get to work, and she didn't want to keep John from doing his job.

"Come on; I'll show you your digs. Jump in with me, and I'll drop you back here later," John said.

Kelsey didn't protest. She would rather drive her own vehicle, but the first rule of every new investigation was to gain as much information as possible. The more she could find out about the town and people, the easier she could do her job. She was from a small town, but that didn't mean she knew the first thing about this one.

She stood with her arms folded across her chest and watched Deputy Gallant slowly get up from the chair, switch off his monitor, and then diligently and methodically put on his jacket and hat. She had expected a cowboy hat, but he wore a woolen beanie. Perhaps he would switch in the summer.

"I guess I have to get used to things moving a lot slower out here," Kelsey sighed.

"We do our jobs," the deputy chafed.

John drove a truck, but she would have guessed that before seeing it—he seemed like that type of guy. She hopped in, and the deputy sheriff drove off more cautiously than she expected.

"World's biggest clothespin," Kelsey murmured as they passed it. It was exactly what it sounded like. A giant wooden clothespin taking pride of place on the side of the main street that ran through town.

"Hey, don't knock it," John said. He briefly lifted his hand to wave to someone outside *Main Street Diner*. "People come from all over to see our landmark, and—"

"Hey, you don't have to sell it to me. World's largest non-operational typewriter. That's where I grew up."

John glanced at her as he drove. "Brought more than just the big city with you," he said.

"Feels familiar," she complained.

Kelsey tried to keep her tone neutral, but she couldn't help but feel it came out as a slight against the town. She had nothing against Winchburgh, just her childhood. She had run from Missouri as fast as she could, and being here made her feel like she had never escaped.

"It's a good town," John boasted. "Good town and good people. Shouldn't have happened." He became sad as he spoke.

"What happened?" she asked.

17

The truck stopped, and John sighed. He looked at her and then out of the window. "Let's finish the tour and then get down to business."

"I'd rather get down to business first," Kelsey said.

"And I was told to show you around first. I heard you were not very good at following orders."

John produced a key from his pocket and dangled it in front of Kelsey.

She grabbed it from him.

"Second floor, number three. You can't miss it." John said. "I'll let you powder your nose or whatever you need to do, but be back here in five minutes."

"There's a difference between following orders and delaying what needs to be done. Whatever happened here is a big deal—I can see it in your face. With a lack of action, that could mean anything. All I will say is, don't get in my way, okay?"

"Five minutes," Deputy Gallant repeated. His expression wavered, but he didn't back down.

As she exited the truck, Kelsey realized she didn't need to go up there just yet; her bags were still in the trunk of her car. Still, she went up to the second floor as quickly as possible, aiming to be back as soon as she checked out where she would be sleeping.

The small apartment was as much as she expected: an open-plan living room and kitchen, one bathroom, and one bedroom. The window overlooked the street, and she glanced at John's black truck idling below. There was nothing else to look at, so she locked back up again and descended the stairs.

The only thing she was worried about was the cold. She had dressed to drive, and her warmer coat and gloves were in her trunk, too. When she got back into the warmth of the truck, John said, "Three minutes and fifteen seconds. Not bad."

"All right, enough of the pleasantries," Kelsey responded. "Are we going to get to work or not?"

John frowned and he immediately looked out of his depth. "I hope so. We might be a tight-knit community, but no one knows who she is or what the hell happened to her."

CHAPTER FOUR

The man stood in the coffee shop and waited for his drink to be made. He studied the barista as she steamed the milk for his cappuccino—Maria was her name if the writing on her badge was correct. He knew that many people nowadays liked to hide their names, both online and in real life. There were a lot of weirdos out there, so he could not blame them.

His gaze did not linger on her name tag for long. He traced the shape of her bust beneath her buttoned white shirt, the small bulge of her midriff above her belt, and the pretty pink ribbon that tied back her hair into a neat ponytail.

He also noticed the chipped nail polish on her nails, the glow of her lipstick or the Chapstick covering the splash of color on her lips, the twinkle in her beautiful blue eyes, the mole on her left cheek, and the way she genuinely smiled at customers—not a fake smile like the ones he had so often seen from almost everyone else in this obtuse world.

The screeching steam was silenced, and Maria gently swirled the foamed milk in the metal pitcher. The espresso cascaded from the machine like two streams of liquid earth, and the milk was expertly poured atop. The result was a chestnut ring around a snow-white circle. Maria placed the lid on top and checked the name on the side of the cup.

"Cappuccino for Grant! I have a cappuccino for Grant!"

Grant stepped forward with a smile. "Thank you, Maria."

Maria stopped mid-turn and looked at him. "How did you—" She burst into a wide, beautiful, enchanting smile and tapped her badge.

Grant did all he could not to look at the gentle bounce of her breasts as she tapped her name tag.

"Duh," Maria continued. "It's right here, Maria!"

So, Maria is your real name!

Grant smiled back at her. "Sorry, I didn't mean to scare you."

"No, it's fine." She laughed again. "Enjoy your cappuccino."

"Oh, Maria, do you happen to have one of those little sticks to place in the little hole to stop the drink from spurting everywhere? I'm driving home and don't want to spill. I forget what they are called."

Maria hesitated for a second, and the slight smile wavered. She quickly regained her composure.

She screwed up the corner of her mouth. "Drink stopper? I think so. Let me grab you one."

She turned and grabbed one from the back counter, giving Grant's gaze another chance to wander without her spotting him checking her out. He didn't want to make her uncomfortable.

"Here you go," she said once she had retrieved one of the small beige stoppers. She handed it to Grant, and he wrapped his hand around hers as he took it. Maria flinched but did not jerk her hand back—she looked too afraid. He looked into her widening eyes and smiled. Maria's response was to quick turn away from him and tackle the next drink. She glanced over at him once before he left—the smile from her face had been wiped, and that excited Grant even more.

Grant walked the three blocks back to his top-floor apartment. When he got there, he had finished the cappuccino. He entered the building to find Mrs. Swallows struggling into the elevator, laden with bags.

"Let me help you with that, Mrs. Swallows," Grant soothed. He ran to catch up with her and take some of the bags.

"Kevin, you are an angel," she said.

"Just doing what I can." He moved his hand to cover the name on the cup. "Isn't it awful that the front door is still broken? Anyone could wander in off the streets."

"Don't!" she warned. "The amount of times I have spoken to someone about that door, and still, nothing is done. It will take a tragedy for them to take action."

"Unfortunately, that is so often the case," the man said.

Like someone being pushed down the stairs by an unknown assailant.

He had often dreamed of giving the old bat the slight nudge it would take to send her toppling down the jagged concrete stairs.

The elevator pinged, and Mrs. Swallows took her bags from him. Her door was opposite the elevator. He watched her put the key in the lock before the doors closed again. When he reached the top floor, he strode confidently to his door and let himself in.

He washed his cup and placed it neatly in the recycling bin atop the others. The caffeine would not stop him from napping. He needed his sleep. He would need all his strength for what was to come. It was almost showtime!

CHAPTER FIVE

"We had to call in some help from the neighboring towns—we've never seen anything like this," John Gallant said.

"I saw them on my way in," Kelsey noted. "Two police cars, an ambulance, and a fire truck. So, what is going on?"

John indicated and waited patiently for the slow car in front of him to turn before he did. Kelsey expected a dead body. The way he drove, spoke, and gave her the quick tour suggested they would see something that was not going anywhere—a dead body. And with the temperature, it would remain fresh for a while.

John tapped on the steering wheel as he drove. "Do you know how people always say it's good to have you here, or you made it just in time, or something like that when someone new comes to town?"

Kelsey nodded.

"Well, we *really* are glad to have you here, and you *really* did get here just in time. We found the body last night, but we think it might have been placed the previous night. I know you think we are all slow and polite around here, but one small sign saying not to uncover the sculpture, and everyone complies. I don't know if it would have helped to find it sooner. I wasn't the one who found it, but I was the first on the scene."

"The Winter Fair," murmured Kelsey.

"Yeah, how did you know?"

"I didn't, but that's about all that's going on in town, right? Makes sense that it was most likely to happen there. And I've noticed how everyone is on edge around here—you can't hide that."

"Yeah, it happened at the Winter Fair," John agreed. "We have an ice sculpture competition every year, and they had set up the sculptures under tarps, but one had been replaced with... well, with a body encased in a block of ice."

"Or it could have been one of the entrants."

John frowned and looked at her quickly before looking back at the road. The deputy sheriff was pretty shaken up about the death and must have expected her to be the same. She had seen worse and read about cases that would cause most people to lose sleep at night. It only drove Kelsey to be better at stopping these same things from happening again.

"Um, yeah." John composed himself. "It could have been an entrant. We've only just started the investigation and didn't want to move the body until you took a look. Do you think it was a man?"

"Stats," Kelsey replied. "It could be a woman, but a death like this feels more violent and needy. If the body is encased in ice, it was done to put on a show or present the body to us. Just feels like it was a man."

"Do they teach you that back in the FBI?" John asked.

"That and more. I'm not here to show you up, Deputy. I'm only here to help, and if we work together, we will get this guy."

John looked impressed. He nodded his head in agreement. "Yeah. Yeah."

It felt good. Back in Quantico and then the field office in Valleyview, she had been on par with the others, even if she was seen as lesser at times. It was different here—she had the most experience and seniority. She had wanted that for the entirety of her short FBI career, but it didn't feel nearly as good as she thought it would. The only thing that would make her feel good in this small town was catching the killer.

It gave her a new purpose.

"Here we are," John announced. He pointed to the large man barking orders at the officers surrounding him. "That's Sheriff Anderson. I'll warn you—he doesn't like outsiders much and hates being undermined. I know you have not come here to do that, but he won't like you being around. The only time I have seen him happy since I took this job is the three weeks between Special Agent Woods leaving for Bismarck and your arrival."

"Don't worry, I can handle myself."

No one could be as bad as her boss back at Valleyview.

"You don't have any idea who she is?" Kelsey asked.

"None of us at the crime scene know her, which means it's unlikely anyone in town will either. She could be from one of the surrounding towns, or she could have been brought from out of state. She's in her late twenties or early thirties and dead. That's all we know. We can get her description out quickly if that's the best thing. We might move slowly around here, but we can get things done quickly when we want."

Kelsey didn't wait for John and exited the vehicle. The sheriff turned and held her gaze for a moment before going back to his officers. She caught some glances from a couple of the officers and members of the public. Not only was she new in a town where everyone knew everybody else, but she was an FBI agent assigned there just as someone was murdered.

John took her arm and held her back. "Let's take a look at the body first and let him get a little more comfortable with you being here before we speak to him."

Kelsey followed John toward the stage at the far end of the deserted Winter Fair. Rides sat motionless, stalls had no people manning them, and tables and chairs remained empty. The stage had yellow tape surrounding it to cordon it off, and two police officers stood at opposite sides to stop members of the public from getting a look.

"The main reason Sheriff Anderson is so pissed right now is that we don't know what this is. Three people were killed almost thirty years ago, but that was discovered to be over a land claim, and the guy was caught pretty quickly," John said.

Kelsey didn't mention the cow from the file that was also killed.

"This is different," John stated. "It's got a lot of us freaked out, and the rest of us are on edge."

"That's understandable."

Kelsey was on edge, too, but not because of the murder. She needed to prove herself, and she had a chance when she thought she would be investigating only the mundane. She would not admit it to anyone, but she was excited.

"You ready?" John asked as they were allowed in by the officer raising the yellow tape.

A unicorn reared up toward the sky, an eagle held its impressive wings out to the side; there was a house that could be entered and a chair to sit on. Those were some of the ice sculptures on display. And then there was one around six feet tall covered with a tarp.

Kelsey nodded.

"Forty years of the Winter Fair and then this," John announced as he pulled the tarp to the side.

The woman was standing up in the ice, arms by her side. Her eyes were glassy and lifeless. Kelsey could feel the suffering. She had been alive when she was placed in the water, and the scream had been frozen, presumably as she drowned. She stared into the eyes some more before looking through the ice to the small patch of opaque white below. It was not snow.

Did you die in the water? Is that why you were screaming? Or did he do something to you first? Kill you and then freeze you? And did he

24

leave a calling card under the ice? Are we dealing with more than just one dead person?

"Cover that up, John. You'll scare the poor girl to death."

Kelsey rolled her eyes and turned to find Sheriff Anderson standing behind her.

"Special Agent Kelsey Barker," Kelsey said with a smile. "You must be Sheriff Anderson."

"Sheriff Anderson," he repeated as if she had pronounced it wrong.

He did not hold out his hand to welcome her, so she did not hold out hers.

"You've probably solved this already with your FBI algorithms and psychoanalysis," the sheriff stated.

"No, we are a long way from that," Kelsey admitted. "I hope we can work together and solve this. This is your town, Sheriff, so I am not going to take control of the investigation." But the implication was that she could. "I'm here in a supporting capacity for now, so whatever you need me for, please let me know."

Sheriff Anderson looked more annoyed than when she and John had pulled up.

"Very kind of you," he stated. "We haven't spoken with Miss Muir yet. Why don't you head to her ranch and ask if she knows anything?"

"Aretha Muir?" John asked. "She's not going to know anything. She's been making ice sculptures for the past fourteen years and pushing eighty. Aretha's the last person who would have anything to do with this."

"I'm sorry," Sheriff Anderson spat, "are you questioning the order?"

"We'll go pay her a visit," Kelsey said, trying to de-escalate the situation. She had dealt with people like this before, and the best way to deal with them was to do what they wanted (and break the rules later). "Deputy, you'll have to show me where the ranch is. I don't want to get lost."

John grimaced, but he didn't put up any more of a fight. He turned and left; Kelsey followed.

She was almost out of earshot when she looked over her shoulder and said, "I presume that as soon as you get the body moved, you'll pick up the card trapped under the ice. It could be nothing, but you never know."

Kelsey didn't wait for a response. She followed quickly after John, and he couldn't hide the small smirk on his face.

"Hey, there is something under there, look!" one of the officers shouted from behind.

"Oh, shut up," Sheriff Anderson snapped.

CHAPTER SIX

"You do realize he sent you out here because he knows you are not going to get any useful information from Miss Muir, right?" John asked.

"Better to follow every single line of inquiry than miss something small," Kelsey responded.

The truck rumbled down the snow-covered dirt road, and Kelsey was glad she was riding in the deputy's truck and not her own vehicle. She was more than capable in most ways, but not when it came to this kind of driving. It was nerve-racking enough to be sitting in the passenger seat.

"So, you have a family?" Kelsey asked, wanting to take her mind off the worry of wiping out and being tossed into a ditch.

"I do." John jerked the steering wheel to the right as they hit another divot in the road. "Married my high-school sweetheart right out of school and then decided to start a family six years ago when I returned from combat. One and done. Not sure what it was, but when Kimberly was born, we were both content to stop there. She's the light of my life—they both are. Must sound pretty boring after living in the big city."

"One combat and done?" Kelsey asked, confused.

"Child," John replied. "No, not one combat. And you? You came here alone, but do you have anyone back home?"

Kelsey didn't know where home was. Mikkisula in Missouri where she had grown up did not feel like home anymore. Valleyview had felt like home from when she had moved there until Darren had cheated on her, and she had run away again. She would have run away to somewhere else if she had not been forced to come here. Now, she was in Winchburgh, which certainly didn't feel like home.

"No," Kelsey murmured. "No one back home."

It was a question that warranted a follow-up, but she was glad that John did not probe further.

"So, you found the body?" Kelsey asked.

She didn't have time to dwell on her past (recent or distant) when there were far more exciting things to think about. Like how she was going to solve this case—that was something that could take her mind off her plethora of problems.

"Yeah, I was at the Winter Fair with Samantha and Kimberly. I heard the scream and went straight to where the body was found after I made sure Kimberly was safe. What you saw today is exactly how it was last night. I mean, no one spotted the card through the ice."

"It might be nothing," Kelsey said.

"It might be something." John smiled.

"What do we have to go on so far?" Kelsey asked. "Eyewitnesses? You don't bring in a block of ice that size without someone seeing something."

"You do when it's a small town like this. New York might be the city that never sleeps, but Winchburgh, North Dakota, is the town that sleeps very soundly between midnight and six a.m. If someone is out during that time, they are likely up to no good. As it turns out, someone was up to no good."

"You know this town, but I don't believe there would be absolutely no one out during those hours. You know who might be up to no good in this town. I want to talk to anyone who might have been out during those hours but doesn't want to admit it. Put some pressure on them, but let them know they won't face any consequences if they were out doing something. Heck, they turn into the town hero if they saw something."

John nodded and tapped the steering wheel. "That's a fricking good idea. I'll get someone to knock on some doors as soon as we get back to town. Some of the businesses in town have CCTV, but not many. The footage should be downloaded from any cameras soon. Other than that, we've no main line of inquiry other than searching who might have hired a truck since they had to have some way to transport the ice block. They maybe had a refrigerated truck, but if it were open, it would have kept the body frozen. However, that's a wider net to cast. Something tells me whoever did this is not from Winchburgh."

"I'm full of *fricking* good ideas." Kelsey shook her head at his small-town timidness, but felt validated to be useful in the inquiry. She could see things the others could not and she thought differently too. It wasn't that the people from the town couldn't do their jobs, but it was always useful to have someone else look at the problem with fresh eyes.

"Something tells me this is not the last we'll see of this guy," Kelsey noted.

John stopped the truck when they pulled up at the small ranch house. He hopped out, and Kelsey followed suit. They were met at the door by an old Black woman. She ushered them in and had some tea waiting. Kelsey was unsure if she had known they were coming or kept a hot pot of tea ready in case anyone might visit.

"I heard the news," she exclaimed. "And you're the new girl, aren't you?"

"Special Agent Kelsey Hawk." Kelsey didn't usually like being called a girl but didn't mind Aretha calling her that.

"They must have me as the prime suspect if they've sent an FBI agent to arrest me," Aretha stated. "Can I at least serve you some tea before you cuff me and take me downtown?"

John chuckled and slapped Aretha playfully on the shoulder. "I should arrest you, but not for this. Anything you can tell us about the ice block we found in the middle of the Winter Fair, Miss Muir?"

Aretha bit her bottom lip and took on a solemn tone. "It's going to rock this town for a long, long time. I've lived here for almost eighty years, and my mother before that. Never has something happened like this." She looked at Kelsey. "You find who did this and find them fast. People won't show it, but everyone is frightened right now. This is the nicest town in the world. How do we expect our children to sleep when something like this might happen again?"

Kelsey nodded glumly. "If it makes you feel any better, it's unlikely that it will happen here again."

"But it could happen somewhere else," Aretha stated. "So, the impetus is still to catch them quickly. It doesn't matter where someone is murdered; it only matters that you can stop it."

Kelsey knew the woman wasn't connected to the murder, but that didn't mean she couldn't be helpful. If Kelsey had learned anything from her time investigating crimes, it was that everyone knew something.

"Miss Muir, you know about ice sculptures. A big block of ice left in the middle of your town - what can you tell me about it?" Kelsey asked.

"A block of ice big enough to house a body," Aretha mused. "It would be very difficult to make that without the right equipment."

"What would you need?" Kelsey asked.

"A mold to hold the water and body," Aretha replied. "A special freezing unit. You could leave it outside if it were cold enough, but only with the right conditions."

"And you would have to do so in a secluded area," John commented.

"All right, so a mold to freeze the ice block and some sort of special freezing equipment. Where would you get something like that?" Kelsey asked.

"I can give you some names that I have used in the past for the equipment I've had."

"Have you checked your equipment?" John asked. "Is it all still there?"

Aretha took a sip of her tea. "I haven't since I carved the eagle, but there's nothing they could take that would be of any use. You are welcome to come and take a look."

"That might be best. Just to put the sheriff's mind at rest," John admitted.

John's radio crackled into life. "Deputy Gallant, come in, please."

"Excuse me," John said. He looked at Kelsey. "You want to check out the equipment, just in case?"

Kelsey nodded.

John headed in one direction, and Aretha led Kelsey in the other. They went through the house and the back door that connected the main residence to the garage. Some equipment was covered by similar tarps to the one that had covered the ice block.

Kelsey felt a chill run down her neck. It could be the cold, or it could be....

She tore the tarps from the equipment and found a chainsaw and other ice-carving equipment.

"Looks like nothing is missing," Aretha stated.

"Hey! We need to move out!" John shouted from inside the house.

Kelsey moved quickly in the direction of the shout.

"Miss Muir, thank you for your time!" John called.

Kelsey followed him outside. "What happened? Have they found him?"

"No." John shook his head. "Another winter festival, another dead body."

CHAPTER SEVEN

"Where are we headed?" Kelsey asked.

"Westerly. It's around thirty clicks from here. Same thing, apparently—they have their own winter festival, much like ours, complete with ice sculptures and the like, and rides and whatnot, and apparently a dead body encased in ice is this season's must-have."

Kelsey knew the deputy sheriff was trying to make light of the situation with a joke, but she couldn't bring herself to laugh. Two bodies in as many days.

One more body than days in my new role. One more body, and we'll have a serial killer on our hands.

Kelsey couldn't help but think a third body was inevitable.

"Let's see if he left any more clues for us." Kelsey hopped back into the black truck. She watched in the side mirror as the ranch receded, Aretha standing in the doorway to watch them leave before closing the door to keep out the cold.

"I want to get as far ahead of this as possible," Kelsey stated. "Who can I use at the sheriff's office to call around for me?"

"If you call now, likely Marcy will answer. She can do any leg work for you," John replied as he turned from the snow-covered dirt road onto the partially icy range road.

"What do I…?"

"Officer Janson," John said.

Kelsey dialed the number she had added to her phone when packing for Winchburgh. It was picked up on the first ring.

"Vanburgh County Sheriff's office, Marcy speaking, how may I assist ya today?"

"Officer Janson, this is Special Agent Kelsey Hawk. I need you to make some calls for me," Kelsey said. She grabbed the small notebook from her bag and flicked through it with her free hand.

"Oh, for sure. Nice to have another woman in town."

"Yeah," Kelsey answered. She had never really thought of herself as just another woman in the justice system. "Listen, can you look into something for me? I have the names of three industrial freezing

31

companies in the area—they all sell and rent equipment and offer freezing solutions."

"Oh, yeah," Marcy said softly—it clicked why she was calling these places.

"Do you have a pen, Officer Janson?"

"One second… got one."

"All right, so we have FrostTech Solutions, PolarIce Molds, and Absolute Zero Freezing. I want to know if they have sold any industrial freezing equipment or molds in the past six months that would produce the block of ice found at the Winter Fair—either as an individual order or part of a larger one. And, Marcy, please be delicate when you are talking to people. We don't need to mention exactly what the equipment might have been used for; so far, anyone who works for these companies or has ordered from them is a suspect, and we don't want to spook them."

"Got it, boss," Marcy replied.

Kelsey thought about correcting her, but she ended the conversation instead. "Thanks, Marcy." She stuffed the phone back in her bag.

"They claim we copied them," John said. He indicated and overtook a blue sedan on the highway.

"What?" Kelsey gazed out the window as the snow-dusted landscape whizzed by in a blur.

"The town of Westerly," John said as if it explained it. Thankfully for Kelsey, he followed it up with, "It's stupid, really, but both towns believe they created the original winter festival. We have the Winter Fair; they have Winterfest. It's not like every single town in the county doesn't have the exact same thing every year."

"Not much else to do out here except squabble over petty things." Kelsey quickly turned to John. "Is it really that much of a big deal?"

"You're still bitter you were sent here. I get it, and don't worry, you don't need to understand people out here. Would sure be a lot better if you did, though."

"Oh, would it? Would it *sure* be better?"

"What the fuck is your problem?" John asked.

"There we go," Kelsey said. "A bit of real emotion. The small-town military man who pussy-foots around with *fricking* this and *aw shucks* that."

John shook his head. "Aw shucks! What a fricking badass you are. Don't worry, I don't take any offense—all of this says much more about you than it does about me."

32

Kelsey was bitter about the relocation and knew it would not subside any time soon. Still, she knew she shouldn't take it out on people doing their jobs and helping her solve this case.

The rest of the drive was made in silence. Kelsey did not want to break it and put her foot in her mouth again, and John was content not to speak. He didn't turn on the radio, perhaps punishing her with the silence.

When they pulled up at the small, deserted winter festival in the town center, Kelsey glanced at John, but she said nothing. They both exited the truck and walked toward a familiar scene: police tape, a large tarp, and several police officers. The only difference was the absence of the sheriff—he had not made the journey out from Winchburgh.

"Never seen anything like this," one of the officers commented when they reached the scene.

"Unfortunately, we have," John said. He gestured toward the tarp. "Let's take a look."

The officer glanced around first to ensure no members of the public had wandered too close. When he was sure no one would see, he lifted the tarp to show the ice block below.

"Same shape, same size," Kelsey commented. "I guarantee this was the same person using the same equipment."

"More peaceful this time," John noted.

The first body screamed through the ice. This one, another female, looked like she was sleeping. Her arms were crossed over her chest in a death pose. Kelsey got closer, half-expecting the corpse within to open its eyes—it remained asleep. She scanned the ground around and through the ice, but there was no card. If it was the killer's card back in Winchburgh, it wasn't a calling card.

"Two bodies in a matter of hours. What sort of sicko does something like this?" John asked.

"That's what we are going to find out," Kelsey replied.

John turned to the officer not holding up the tarp. "I'm sure you are checking CCTV, talking to people, all that stuff. If you find anything, I want you to call me."

The officer nodded.

Kelsey slowly turned in a circle, taking in what she could see of the town and the mountains behind. It all looked so peaceful. John was right. What sort of sicko would do something like this, and why here? Why in Winchburgh? Why leave them like this? It was a display, a game, a need of the killer—she was sure of that. He was compelled to do this for some reason.

Find the killer; find out why. Find the why, find the killer.

Kelsey's phone rang.

"Hey," she answered.

"So, I called the three companies you told me to," Marcy said, "FrostTech is closed and has been for the past eight months. I don't have any information on why that was or what happened to them. PolarIce sells molds but only used ones, and the equipment they have is likely not big enough. In any case, they only rent freezing equipment; they don't sell it, except for the molds. Absolute Zero is your best bet. I'm sending the address to you now. If you're in Westerly, you only have to drive another twenty miles to talk with them over there."

"Thank you, Marcy. That helps a lot. Listen, can you follow up with FrostTech and see if they still have equipment on the premises—maybe someone broke in, or an ex-employee took some stuff. And get a list of the equipment PolarIce has rented out. If no one has already, start going through any missing persons reports in the past three months—focus on women only for now.

"Will do."

"Thanks, Marcy. Bye."

"What do we have?" John asked.

"A potential lead. We need to go to"—Kelsey checked the message on her phone—"Inishale. You up for a road trip?"

"What's in Inishale?" John asked.

"Either the killer or someone who might have interacted with him recently."

CHAPTER EIGHT

"Does it just get colder here the farther you drive?" Kelsey asked. "It feels like every new town we go to is colder than the last."

"You'll get used to it."

"I don't know if I'll ever get used to this," Kelsey replied.

Even in the warmth of John's truck, Kelsey felt chilled to the bone. It was the kind of cold that came from inside, not outside. She felt she would not have peace from the chill in her bones until she caught this guy.

"It's like the whole state is trying its best to be a picturesque winter postcard. Look, *another* frozen lake." Kelsey pointed out the window.

It was the tenth one they had passed since they had been driving. When she entered the state, the first few she had seen had been charming, but it became tiresome when every lake was frozen. She was used to swimming in lakes or water skiing. There wasn't any of that here.

"Don't worry, they thaw in the summer," John said.

"We need to catch him by then. He needs the cold for his multiple tableaus. It will not be good if we don't catch him by the time the thaw comes. Either he stops and disappears or has time to plan for the next winter—two dead bodies already, Deputy. We both know more are to come. There's something with the cold, the winter. Maybe the ice show. He has memories of the winter festivals. It's deliberate—there's some psychosis."

"We know he's a psychopath."

"He is, but that doesn't mean he's completely insane. He's killed two women already, and if he's done so in quick succession, he might bide his time before the next one, but he will be thinking about his next kill. Two bodies, frozen in ice and placed in full view. I don't think that's reckless. He is clever—he knows he can be brazen and get away with it. For now."

"What if we don't catch him?" John asked.

"We will."

35

John looked ahead at the empty open road as he drove. There were mountains in the distance topped with snow. No matter which way Kelsey looked, there seemed to be snow-topped mountains, cold radiating down from them. Snow ghosts weaved back and forth across the highway as the breeze picked up the loose snow from the drifts on either side. Snow covered the fields—green had become white for five months. It was suffocating.

"It could be the guy we are going to see," John said.

"I really hope it is, but my gut tells me it's not him. If this guy is as clever as I think he is, he won't leave a trail for us. There are two types of killers in the world: those who want to be caught and those who don't. This guy wants us to see his work—we are the audience to his show—but he doesn't want to be caught. He will continue to do this until he is caught, but he doesn't *want* to be caught. Would he sell the equipment used to freeze the bodies? I don't think he's that stupid."

"Then what are we doing out here?" John asked.

"I love to be right, Deputy, but if it means catching a killer, I don't mind being wrong. That's another thing I've learned from my time in the FBI—stupidity is often mistaken for intelligence. We had a case a couple of years ago with children being kidnapped. It looked like the two guys behind it had planned everything meticulously, but it turned out that they were grabbing random kids, and we saw a pattern that wasn't there. We got them in the end through luck, but it took longer than it should have—good luck for them and bad for us. So, while I'm convinced this guy is not our guy, let's hope he's relying on stupid good luck, and he's an idiot."

Kelsey tapped her fingers on the door handle. They passed a sign as they neared the town:

Inishale 2 Miles

City of Bridges 17 Miles

"City of Bridges," Kelsey said. "I read up about that when I was packing to move out here. One of the top ten tourist attractions in North Dakota. Is it really worth a visit? It's like, a load of bridges, right?"

"Yeah," John laughed. "It's hard to explain, but it's a place that draws you in. It doesn't sound like much when you put it like that, but you have to experience it. Don't worry; it'll draw you in sooner or later. Beautiful in both the winter and summer."

"And it's not a city, right?" Kelsey asked.

"No, but the Town of Bridges doesn't quite have the same ring to it. I go there with the family sometimes. There's a great walk that takes you over all the bridges. Seventeen of them!"

"Maybe I'll wait until summer to check it out."

The thought depressed Kelsey. That meant she was here until the summer and who knew how long after that. She didn't want to be here at all. If she kept her head down and did her job, she might get a move out of this place. She didn't care where she went after this as long as it was warm. She shivered as the car pulled up outside Absolute Zero.

"Hold on," John said as Kelsey reached for the handle. "Look, it's closed."

"The hours on the website said they were open."

"Yeah, but look." John pointed to the adjoining building: a butcher. "No one in a small town has one job. There's not enough to go around. I guarantee you that the guy who owns Absolute Zero also owns Meat & Stuff. Makes sense. There will be a meat freezer, and they'll share facilities. Maybe space to store a body."

"Okay, we can work with that."

"Wait," John said slowly as Kelsey reached for the handle again. "I know guys like this. I guarantee he's going to be creepy as heck, and he'll likely come out the back with a blood-soaked apron and a big cleaver, and he'll just be weird. Whatever you do, don't ask him anything about his job."

"That's going to be pretty hard."

"Hey, don't say I didn't warn you."

They both got out, and Kelsey pulled out her phone to check the information Marcy had sent over. The guy's name was Ernie Wall, and there was no mention of a butcher's shop. Just having her phone out for fifteen seconds froze her fingers, and she jammed them back into her pockets.

They went to Absolute Zero first and looked inside. It was dark, and the door was locked when they tried it, but they could see shelves of equipment and large-scale freezers as far as the light allowed. There was no sign on the door, no indication that they should go into the butcher's if they wanted to gain access.

Kelsey looked around, and the entire town looked dead. She hoped it was only the cold keeping people inside. She tried the butcher's door and found it unlocked. They entered together. There was a distinct smell of bleach inside. The square floor tiles and rectangular wall tiles were as white as the snow outside. John moved as if he were following the straight lines on the floor, starting close to the side wall with a view of the front door.

A small black radio with a crooked metal antenna crackled on top of the glass display case. Inside, small slabs of meat were stacked on top of each other, surrounded by ice. They were neat and clean, bright bloody red against the white. Kelsey looked at John, and he shrugged in response.

It was almost as cold in the butcher's as it was outside. The cold attacked them from both sides, seeping through the door they had come through and also coming from the large walk-in freezer behind the counter. Kelsey nodded toward the large door.

She placed her hand on the gun attached to her belt and went into the large freezer first. John didn't reach for his weapon, but he did mirror her speed as they moved past the counter and into the freezer. The cold hit her, but it was a different type of cold than the iciness outside. It was the same cold that ran through her bones, and she felt like one of the victims.

Did they feel anything as they were killed?

She was too determined to have been scared of what she was walking into.

Large pieces of animals hung on meat hooks from the ceiling, and they swung back and forth gently, obscuring the view to the back, where a rhythmic thud sounded.

"Hello?" Kelsey called.

The thudding stopped. Condensation filled the air like fog. Kelsey felt a presence but only saw the shadow of a man. He emerged through the mist and stood before them. His forearms were bare and thick, his tough brown leather apron stained black, and blood dripped from his cleaver to freeze on the floor before it had a chance to congeal.

Kelsey looked down and realized the entire floor was blood red.

CHAPTER NINE

"Mr. Wall?" Kelsey asked, hand still on her gun in its holster.

"Yeah, what are you doing back here?"

"Mr. Wall, I'm Special Agent Kelsey Hawk with the FBI. I will show you my badge, but I need you to put down the cleaver first."

Ernie Wall looked down at Kelsey's gun, and he frowned. For a moment, she did not think he was going to comply, but he eventually held up his other hand and turned and walked away before she could stop him.

For a moment, Ernie disappeared, but his shadow reappeared a second later, and Kelsey felt the hairs prickle on the back of her neck. She readied herself to draw her gun if he lunged at her, but he reappeared almost the same as before—only minus the cleaver this time.

She relaxed as much as she could in a walk-in freezer. "You own this place, Mr. Wall?"

There was an audible sigh from behind, and a cloud of breath pushed past her and up into the ceiling.

"It's more than just a job," Ernie said. "I'm helping them pass into the next life. You're not from around here, are you?"

Kelsey didn't answer—she let him speak instead.

"This freezer is the connection of life to death. They might be dead when I bring them in here, but that does not mean the life is gone. It takes a lot of skill to cut flesh from bone, dissect sinews and organs, to detach the skin from a beast so it can be used to give life somewhere else—can be used to honor the fallen animal. Course, you won't see any of this, will you? Go to the grocery store and grab a pack of meat, a rough-hewn slab of flesh wrenched from a carcass. It takes a skilled hand to cut meat and not flesh. Just as my father before me and my grandfather before him have done, so do I. It takes the sharpest knife to cut, but the dullest hand will massacre. I can see their souls dance in here when I cut through the skin, separate bone from bone. You won't ever get that, Special Agent, and I pity you."

"We are talking about animals, aren't we?" Kelsey asked.

"I don't see them as animals," Ernie replied.

"We need to ask you a few questions, Mr. Wall. Would you mind stepping out of the freezer with Deputy Gallant?"

Ernie held Kelsey's gaze for a second before his eyes flickered to the back of the room, the part still obscured by the chill mist.

"I don't know what you are looking for, but you won't find it here." Ernie didn't wait to be led out. He walked toward the large freezer door and pushed it open.

John gave her an I-told-you-so look and shook his head before following Ernie out of the large ice box. Kelsey still had her hand on her gun, and she kept it there as she gingerly walked toward the back of the freezer. The hunks of hanging meat danced around her, and it was as if they whispered to her as they passed. Perhaps their souls were trapped in the freezer with her.

The cold was gone, or perhaps she was used to it.

Did it feel like this? Did they slip away gently?

The frozen scream of the first body suggested they did not.

Kelsey mentally pushed through the parts of dead animals swaying around her and approached the back of the room. There was a table, and atop it was a dead body: a partially dissected deer. It stared at her with glassy eyes, the same look as the woman screaming at her from within the ice. Kelsey took one final look around and left the cold to rejoin John.

"Did you see her?" Ernie asked once Kelsey was in the relative warmth of the retail area.

"The deer?" Kelsey asked.

Ernie nodded.

"Mr. Wall, where were you two nights ago?" Kelsey asked, getting straight to the point.

"Two nights ago? Yeah, probably at home. I can check my calendar. The deer is legit, by the way. My friend has a hunting license."

Ernie was a little less weird and creepy now that he was not on his home turf—Kelsey could see he was most comfortable in the freezer with his apron and cleaver. Out here, he was just a regular guy.

"I suggest you check your calendar right now, and we need to see logs of any industrial freezing equipment you have sold over the past six months. Do you have any employees?"

"Um, yeah, I have a kid who comes in and helps me on a Saturday sometimes."

40

"I will need his number, too."

Where creepiness once was, there was now concern.

"Am I in some sort of trouble?" Ernie asked.

"That's what we are here to find out. We have two dead bodies, Mr. Wall. Both were frozen in blocks of ice after they were killed. Now, you have a butcher shop with a walk-in freezer and run a company that sells freezing equipment. Do you see where I am going with this?"

Ernie shook his head, and he was transformed into a little boy. "I had nothing to do with anything. I didn't kill anyone, I promise. And I'll get you receipts of the equipment I've sold, but business hasn't been all that good, and I supply the locals around here for what they hunt. I could probably give you a list of customers off the top of my head, but I've sold nothing that could do what you say."

"Then you have nothing to worry about," Kelsey said. "So, if you could get those receipts and check where you were that night, we can quickly get out of your hair."

There was still something suspicious about the butcher, but Kelsey couldn't pinpoint what it was.

"We should go through to next door. I can close this place down for lunch while I get you what you need," Ernie said.

"The floor was covered in blood back there," Kelsey noted as she followed Ernie out of the store.

"Yeah, there's blood. I, uh, scrape it all off weekly and dispose of it. It looks bad because of the color, but it's not really all that much."

"Would you be okay with us testing some of it, Mr. Wall?" Kelsey asked.

It was a long shot as there were no visible wounds on the victim, but she had to be thorough. If there was any of the victim's DNA here, they couldn't risk losing it.

"Yeah, of course. You can test whenever you want. I've got nothing to hide." He fumbled the keys to the door.

Kelsey's phone buzzed. She checked the screen; it was the sheriff's office.

"Get me an alibi, all the receipts he has, and I want any security footage from that night and the weeks preceding it. Start on the night itself and work your way back. I'll be there in a second," Kelsey told John.

She answered the phone. "Hello?"

"Hi, Kelsey; it's Marcy."

"What do you have for me, Marcy?"

"Okay, so they removed the body from the crime scene and are defrosting it slowly so there won't be any tissue damage. They'll start the autopsy later today, and they are bringing the other body down. It's almost cold enough out that they don't need a refrigerated truck."

"You didn't call with just that, did you? I'm with a suspect, so tell me what you have, Marcy."

"Oh, for sure. So, when they removed the ice block, they found a card under it, just like you said. It's for a coffee place in Bismarck— *Cappa's*. Not a chain, just the one place."

"All right, that's great work, Marcy. What I want you to do is call Special Agent Trevor Wood. He's working on a case in Bismarck. See if you can get him to go and talk to them. I don't know if they will have anything or if it belongs to the killer, but you never know. Every little bit helps, right?"

"You got it, boss. I'll get on it right away."

"Thanks, Marcy."

Kelsey hung up the phone and stood outside the store for a few minutes, taking in the cold. If she built up her tolerance, maybe she could weather this state. When her thighs started to get cold, she went inside and through to the back of the store. She found the deputy and Ernie Wall in a small office.

"He has an alibi," John said.

"I was with my wife and kids all night. We even had some people over, and my daughter had a sleepover with a few friends. I have it on my calendar."

Kelsey almost found it funny that the guy she had met in the freezer with a bloody apron and cleaver was a family man whose daughter had sleepovers.

"All right. We'll need to speak to them to confirm this, so get everyone's numbers, as well as the number of the kid who works for you. How are we doing with the receipts?"

"I can give them to you now; it's just a few boxes, but…."

Kelsey turned to John, who was sitting at the desk. "What's going on?"

"You are going to want to see this," John said. "I did as you asked with the footage. Nothing for last night or two nights ago, but this is interesting. Four nights previous, around two a.m., a car pulls up, and two people enter the building."

"What did they steal?" Kelsey asked.

"It looks like they stole nothing, but I'm pretty sure one is our killer," John said.

"What makes you think that?"

"Well, two people went in, but only one came out alive."

CHAPTER TEN

The phone rang and rang. It rang ten times before the electronic answering machine kicked in.

"Hello? Yes, I can't come to the phone right now, but please leave me a message, and I will get back to you as soon as I can."

There was a shrill beeping tone.

"Hello, Grammy. It's me again. I am just checking in for another week. You can call me if you like, but I understand if you can't. I guess you are sleeping. Anyway, I wanted you to know that I am doing well and will see a girl later. I can already hear your voice, Grammy. I am not going to talk with her about marriage. We haven't even been on our first date yet. I will call you as soon as I get back in and let you know how it went. And I will be on my very best behavior. A gentleman is a gentleman forever. Okay, Grammy, call me if you can. I need to go. I love you."

The man pressed the tactile button on his flip phone to hang up, and he folded it closed. He placed it on the table and smiled at the device.

"Happy now, you little old bitch?"

The man quickly rose from the plush leather chair and rushed to the bathroom. He flipped up the toilet seat and got down on his knees. His abdomen forced out the contents—a little food, but mainly the bile that had settled in the pit of his stomach over the years. He wretched a few final times as nothing more came out. When he was done, he groaned and tore off two pieces of toilet paper to wipe his mouth. He flushed the soiled toilet paper with his vomit. He carefully washed his hands, singing Happy Birthday to himself twice.

It wasn't his birthday for another two months, but he looked forward to it. He would do something special—treat himself.

"Well, get a hold of yourself! You want to look your best for your lady, right?"

He looked at his reflection in the mirror.

"What if I am not good enough for her?"

"You are good enough for anyone. She is going to love you."

"Love me? Steady on there, buddy. We should take things slow, shouldn't we?"

"Only as slow as we need to. If she likes you, we shouldn't hold back. You want her to be happy, don't you?"

"Of course."

"Well, there you go. Go on, go, and get ready and put on your dancing clothes! Hey, this could be the one."

The man smiled at himself in the mirror but quickly looked away. He didn't want to look himself in the eyes anymore. He wished for her to be the one, but he was used to disappointment. There had been other women, but they were not as special as he'd hoped.

He heard a whisper from over his shoulder. "Don't give up. You will find your soulmate."

The man almost cried, but he didn't let himself. He was stronger than that and didn't want the cold to come. He pursed his lips and breathed in deeply through his flared nostrils. He stood with his back to the mirror and wanted to turn and embrace that voice, but if he did, he might lose his nerve and not venture out on his date. There was no time to lose, and he had a long way to travel this evening.

He went straight to the bedroom. The socks in the laundry basket were not folded properly, and he had to take another deep breath. If he started missing things like that, then what was next? Everything needed order, and life made sense when all was in its place. He quickly folded the socks before he got ready for his evening.

His grandmother would tell him to wear a suit, but she was old-fashioned like that. He chuckled as he thought of turning up for a simple date in a full suit. He would look ridiculous.

Instead, he opted for a pair of black slacks and a gray t-shirt. He looked at himself in the mirror—the afternoons at the gym were working, and he was physically and mentally stronger than before. He looked himself up and down. He looked good.

The man went downstairs and walked a block to his car. It was difficult to find parking right outside the building, but he didn't mind the walk in the cold. It invigorated him. It was almost a two-hour drive to the café.

"Don't worry, my dear. You are worth it," he said as he got into the car.

He pulled away from the curb and started the long journey. It was rush hour, but it would be smooth sailing once he got out of the city. Cars honked in an orchestrated concerto around him. He never understood why people were so angry. They needed a cold bucket of water poured on them to cool their tempers. He laughed at the thought of an adult drenched in cold water, the moisture slowly freezing to create icicles in their hair and eyelashes.

He left the city behind, the lights visible in the rearview mirror for a while before disappearing. Then it was darkness. Not the usual darkness of night but the suffocating darkness of winter. It was still early, but the sun and moon did not care. When he reached the small town, he felt more at home than in the city. The people were different here.

The man rechecked the directions and made his way to the café. When he exited the car, he saw her sitting in the café window. She was just as beautiful as he remembered, though she wore a pink blouse this time instead of the green one she had worn on the three previous occasions.

The bench on the other side of the street faced the window, and he sat there to think. He watched as she ordered a glass of wine. Her lips were almost as ruby as the merlot within. She had the fish for her main course, skipping a starter, and some chocolate cake for dessert. She wiped the chocolate from her lips, taking some lipstick with it.

He smiled and wiped his lips with a handkerchief.

Finding her was serendipitous. He had been out on one of his expeditions around the small towns in the area and had spotted her in a window. A little window shopping: he had laughed about that at the time. Then, when he came back the next week, she had been sitting there again, waiting for him. He did not often put in as much effort, but she was worth it, and if she was as predictable as she had been, he could turn his thoughts to others.

She was so lonely, and he wanted to ensure she was no longer lonely.

When she was done, she paid the bill with a smile. It was a beautiful smile. He committed it to memory. He did not get up from the bench until she was almost around the corner. Then he followed her, keeping his distance the entire time. The night was brisk, but he didn't feel the cold in his gray t-shirt. He watched her enter the small townhouse, standing across from it in the shadows. He could not see her through the window when the light went on upstairs, but he knew she was up there.

He waited. He watched the house for hours as lights turned on and off in different rooms. He lived her life in his mind. Finally, the upstairs light was the only one left on. The moon was high and bright in the sky when it went out, shrouding the house in darkness.

The man rubbed a hand over his mouth. "Goodnight," he whispered. "We will be together soon. I promise."

CHAPTER ELEVEN

Kelsey watched the entire thing. The timestamp on the bottom corner of the small monitor said 2:04 a.m. The date showed it was from four nights ago. The footage showed the back of the building. The car pulled up and stopped with only the front of the hood in view. A moment later, two figures entered the scene. One was facing away from the camera, not wanting to be seen. They were pushing another figure who was bound and hooded. They disappeared from the shot.

"That's all we see until... two hours later," John said, fast-forwarding through the footage. "Then, he comes out carrying her. It has to be her, right?"

Kelsey's eyes were glued to the screen as the figure emerged from the back of the building carrying something around five and a half feet in length. It was covered in black garbage bags and was rigid. It was the woman's dead body they had found screaming in the ice. Kelsey had no doubt in her mind that the killer had killed a victim here; she just did not know why.

"Wind it back," she said. "This is the first picture we have of our killer."

"What?" Ernie placed a hand against the shelving unit in the office and breathed in short gasps. "I'll get the phone numbers, I promise. I had nothing to do with this—you have to believe me. How did they even get in? We've not had any break-ins here ever. I don't know what this is; you have to believe me. I'll do anything you need."

"Ernie, take a breath," Kelsey said. "I believe you, but we will have to take you in for more questioning, all right? Deputy, get on the phone and get a team down here as quickly as possible. If he was here, there might be something."

"You don't think there will be, do you?" John asked.

"He's brave, but he's meticulous. He left us nothing at the crime scenes unless the card under the ice is his. And, if he broke into this place and left it as if no one had been here, then he's good. It also means he might know this place. Ernie, how far back do your receipts go?"

"Maybe eighteen months. We don't have to legally keep them for any time, so I toss 'em after the tax year is over."

"Give me what you have. Do you remember selling big units over the past few years?" Kelsey asked.

"I... I don't know. I can try and remember, but I can't account for everything."

"Just do your best. Whatever you have will be helpful."

"And if I can't remember, I am letting other people die, right?"

Kelsey gestured for John to get out of there and start making some calls.

"Ernie, how about you show me which of the units you have here could be used to freeze an animal carcass quickly."

Ernie nodded and rubbed a hand over his nose and mouth. Kelsey looked back at the screen before she left.

"Hey, Ernie, can you zoom in on this thing?"

"Um, yeah, I think so. Let me take a look."

Kelsey looked at the frozen picture of the man carrying the frozen dead body. "Zoom in on the shoes if you can. Do they look unusual to you?"

It wasn't a question to be answered, and Kelsey was glad when he didn't. He tapped a few buttons on the keyboard, and the grainy image zoomed in to show shoes with vibrant colors and some writing on the side. The image was too grainy for the writing to be made out, but that was not what caught Kelsey's eye.

The letters glowed in the dark.

The man wore almost all black, but the shoes were bright—a stark contrast.

You want to be seen, don't you? Not just in what you present to us. You want people to see you in your daily routine because you've spent so long in the shadows. Well, I see you, and I'm coming for you.

"Leave that as it is for now," Kelsey ordered. "Take me to the units he might have used."

Ernie nodded, but he was dazed. He looked at the screen and back at Kelsey. He was still coming to terms with the fact that someone might have been killed in his building. She might sympathize with him if she had the capacity. All she cared about was getting this guy before he killed again, and if she couldn't do that, then she would limit how many people he killed.

"Um, right this way," Ernie said.

49

He had been big and fierce in the freezer but shrunk before her. Ernie led her through to the display area and pointed at a few units.

"Maybe this one and that one over there, but the one in the corner is a heavy-duty one. If you wanted to freeze an animal quickly, that's the one you would use."

"And how long does it take to get down to temperature?"

"It doesn't. All the big units, I keep them plugged in. That way, I can demonstrate them to the customers. It saves on energy. Once they are plugged in, and at temperature, they don't use much power. It's the cooling down part that drains more."

"We're going to have to scour this place, Ernie. You won't be open for a few days—this is an active crime scene now. We will take you to the local police station for a formal statement once the team gets here, but don't worry about that, okay?"

"I… just… yeah, whatever I can do. Can I have my one phone call?" Ernie asked.

Kelsey smiled. "You are not under arrest. Why don't you go and call your family and let them know what is happening? Tell them not to worry. You can get me those phone numbers at the same time. I'd prefer it if you didn't go back into the office for now, and I would like you to stay on the premises until the team gets here. Can you do that for me?"

"Yeah, yeah," he said.

Ernie pulled out his phone and made a call. He walked around the immediate vicinity, staying away from the three units he had pointed out. John returned from the outside a minute later.

"They will be here within the hour," the deputy said. "Damn! If someone had seen something, we could have caught him. Do you think he actually killed her in here?"

"I think he did. For some reason, he needed to come here, and he knew he might be caught. I think he knew about this place already. Maybe this is where he got his equipment from, so he knew there was equipment here, or maybe he cased the place as a potential customer."

"Why would he come here to use the equipment if he has his own? Should we start calling around other places like this? Check the security footage in town close to where the second body was found?"

"Yes," Kelsey said slowly.

The deputy put his hands on his hips. "You don't think we will find anything, do you? We found something here."

"This was a lucky break. We thought he might have bought equipment here, not used the place. He was never meant to be here—it's too public. No, he's too careful, but he's also determined. Something happened that night or that day. He couldn't kill her like he wanted. I think he killed his first here but will have killed the second at his place."

"His place?"

"He has a place where he can take them and kill them. But he couldn't use it for the first victim. Maybe the second one was already there?"

"What if he wasn't set up for it yet?" the deputy asked.

"No, that doesn't make sense. He planned these kills. I know the answer is there; I just need to find it."

Kelsey berated herself for not having the answer. Her mind was working overtime to try and piece together everything she knew about him, but it was not working fast enough. It frustrated her. If she didn't find him, he would kill again.

"Let's forget about that for now," she said, partly to herself and partly to John. "We have a picture of this guy and a lead we can follow. We know he likes to create a scene. I think he likes to show off a little in his regular life. He's the kind of guy who wears a suit but pairs it with sneakers or a plain jacket with a loud scarf. You know that type of thing? So, you'll find a zoomed-in image of his shoes in the office. I can't make them out, but I'm sure the writing on them glows in the dark. Get the video to the lab and see if they can enhance it. I doubt they will be able to, but we might not need that. You were the one who found the body, right?"

"Yeah, I was at Winter Fair," John replied.

"I think he might have been there too. He created the scene for us to discover, but he would have wanted to see the body being discovered—experience the thrill of it. This was his grisly art spectacle. I want you to get everyone available to check any CCTV from the evening before the body was discovered. Every angle of Winter Fair. He was there to leave the body but returned to watch the reveal. We don't know what he looks like, but we might spot him if he has the same shoes on. If we can see his face, we can catch him."

51

CHAPTER TWELVE

Another trip in the truck, but this time it wasn't to another town. The entire freezing equipment store and butcher's shop were being scoured by forensics, and Ernie Wall had been taken back to the local station for follow-up questions. Kelsey wanted to be the one to question him, but there were other places to be. She didn't mind that too much. She was willing to stake her reputation that he wasn't the one behind this. One look at the figure caught on CCTV told her that. Ernie Wall was a big man, and while the man in the footage was tall and strong, he didn't have the same large gut as Ernie.

Where does that leave us? A coffee card from Bismarck that may or may not be the killer's, a man who likely had his own setup but wasn't afraid to adapt, most likely a loner, but trying to fit in, likely charismatic, someone with trauma in their life, someone who wanted to be seen by society.

It was a good profile, but it didn't help them catch the killer yet.

Kelsey's phone rang. She checked the number on the screen, and her heart missed a beat. It wasn't her old SAC, but the call came from her old office. She didn't know whether she should pick up or not. When John shot her another glance, she decided to answer the phone.

"Hello?"

"Kelsey, how are you doing?"

"Mandy?"

"Are you freezing your ass off out there?"

Kelsey tried to make sense of it. She wasn't sure she had any real friends back in the old office, but special Agent Amanda Briggins was possibly the closest she got.

"Um, yeah, something like that."

She didn't like the place, but she felt weird saying that over the phone now that she was there. She had to prove to them that she could survive and thrive in any climate.

"Sorry, yeah," Kelsey added when there was silence. "I'm doing all right out here. I presume you've heard about the case."

"Seems like trouble follows you," Mandy commented.

"Or I follow it. Is that why you are calling? Do you have something connected to the case?"

"Yes, and no," she replied. "SAC Granger is following your progress out there."

"What? Why?"

"He doesn't talk about it, obviously, but if you ask me, he was hoping that you would either refuse the position or leave it once you discovered how nothing happens out there. Then you go and stumble on the biggest case in the area for the past... well, there's never been anything like that out there. He's pretty annoyed, Kelsey."

"He can go screw himself," Kelsey said.

That elicited a quick glance and a smile from John in the driver's seat.

"Yeah, he probably can, but I just thought I would warn you. I've heard stories about him and the agents he doesn't like, and he's forced out about half a dozen. The worst possible thing you could have done is go out there and do your job well. Hell, if you actually catch this guy, he's really going to come for you."

"I don't get what his problem is." Kelsey looked out at the snow-covered streets. The roads had been salted and plowed multiple times, creating large banks of dirty snow on either side. The grittiness matched how she felt inside.

"He's proud, Kelsey. He didn't like you coming in and disobeying orders, and I understand why you did, but you got under his skin. He managed to get you transferred, citing that you were disobedient or not good at your job or some shit, and if you prove him wrong on that, he won't lose the grudge. I just thought you should know that there's some chatter about you back here, so watch your back."

"Thanks, Mandy. How is everything going?"

"The killers don't have time to encase victims in ice—it's been hot every day since you left. Apart from that, it's too quiet and organized here. You might have been a troublemaker, but the fun kind. It's less exciting, and there's no one who's taking the fight to the bad guys. We get there, just through a lot of red tape and even more since you left."

"Hey, at least I left a legacy. Listen, we are almost at a suspect's house. Can we talk again sometime?"

"Yeah, I would like that," Mandy replied.

"And if you ever get sick of the heat, you can come out here and cool down."

"Oh, screw that! You're on your own out there."

Kelsey laughed and said goodbye. As soon as she hung up, her mood turned as dark as the approaching storm. It was visible above the mountains in the distance and slowly rolling in toward the town. Rich, gray clouds tinged with purple and green. The wind was picking up—thunder and lightning were on the way.

"Don't worry, we're not in for any hail," John said as he looked ahead.

"I wasn't worried about that; I'm more worried about snow."

"Oh, we are definitely getting more snow—I'm just worried about us having to bunker in town. With this case, something tells me that we will be stretched all over the area, and it takes time to clear the roads if the snow is heavy."

"Great," Kelsey sighed,

She picked up the blurry picture Marcy had printed off back at the office. It showed a vague figure of what could be presumed a man, and if you squinted at his shoes, they looked similar to the ones the killer had worn.

"You're sure this is the guy?" Kelsey asked.

"No, but it's all we have. You've been through the footage too. We can't be sure, but that's the best match. I don't know if I've ever seen shoes like that."

"And you saw him that night?"

"Yeah, I saw *him*, but I don't remember the shoes. You can see the large camera by his side. Yeah, it's blurry, too, but no one else carries around equipment like that. No one I know of. It has to be Frank."

"And he works for the police department?" Kelsey asked.

"Yes. I mean, not officially. You know what it's like in a small town like this." John looked at Kelsey and chuckled. "No, you probably don't. We don't have the budget to cover everything, and you saw back with Ernie Wall that most people work more than one job. Frank has a good camera, so he gets called on to take photos. That includes crime scene photos." John shook his head. "Don't look at me like that. Before this case, we were talking about burglaries and that kind of thing. He's never photographed a dead body or anything like that."

"And he was there on the night the body was discovered with his camera."

"Yes."

"So, he might have been there to photograph the scene."

"He was there to photograph the Winter Fair. The city employed him for the week to take photos of everything. Look, I'm not saying he didn't do this, but he was at my brother's wedding as the wedding photographer. Everyone in town knows him, and he doesn't fit your profile. I'm not trying to prove his innocence, but I know the people here. You might have your fancy FBI profiling, but everyone in a small town will seem weird to you until you get to know them."

"I know you, Deputy, and you are the weirdest."

John burst out laughing, and Kelsey joined him. All the pent-up aggression, frustration, and anger had bubbled to the surface, and it was the only way to relieve some of it.

"I'm learning," Kelsey said when the laughter died down. "It's nice to have your local knowledge. It feels like everyone is family here, and families can't hide things well from each other."

"How about your family?" John asked. "Are they out here? Is that why you came, or are they back where it's hot? I feel like I don't know anything about you."

"You don't need to," Kelsey said angrily.

John didn't reply, but he did let out a small scoff.

Kelsey rubbed her head before reaching for the door handle. She didn't need to let anyone get close to her out here. The closer they were, the more she had to lose.

"They're dead. All right," Kelsey said before they exited the vehicle. "Can we just leave it at that?"

"I'm sorry," John said softly. "I didn't know. If there is any—"

"No, there's nothing you can do to help. It was a long time ago, and I'd like it to stay in the past."

John looked like he wanted to say something more but remained silent.

They got out of the truck and walked silently up to the house. John looked at Kelsey, and she gestured toward the door. He knocked. A moment later, a middle-aged woman answered the door. She had a welcoming smile and warm eyes.

"Deputy," she said. She looked at Kelsey with wariness.

"Dawn, is Frank home? We tried him at his studio, but no one in the neighboring businesses has seen him in a couple of days," John said.

"He, eh, has not been feeling well lately."

Kelsey could tell that the woman was hiding something.

"Not been feeling well, or not himself?" Kelsey asked.

"I... I don't know. You should speak to him," Dawn said.

"Is he in?" John asked.

"No," Dawn replied, tears welling. "He's not usually gone this long."

"This long? What does that mean?" Kelsey asked.

"He sometimes gets like this. He gets depressed or manic and goes out for a drive, but he's usually only gone for an hour or so."

"When was the last time you saw him?" John asked.

"This morning. Oh, I was going to call it in, but he can't be missing." Dawn started to sob.

John placed a hand on her shoulder. "Hey, it's going to be fine. We are going to find him and bring him back to you. Do you have any idea where he might have gone?"

"I don't... sometimes, he likes to drive out on the Enchanted Highway."

"Okay, that's good. We'll go out there right now," John said calmly. He smiled at Dawn. "If you hear from him, give me a call, all right?"

"I will," she muttered.

John pulled Kelsey away from the door and quickly walked back to the truck. As soon as the door was closed, he looked up toward the storm.

"We need to get out there while we still can. We have to find him before it's too late."

CHAPTER THIRTEEN

"The Enchanted Highway," Kelsey said. "I don't like the sound of that. People go missing? Witchcraft? Weird occurrences? You think something's going to happen to him out there?"

"Do you believe in all of that?" John asked as he drove.

"No, but I believe it can be used to cover the truth, and the truth is usually much worse, so better to believe in the supernatural than people doing bad things."

"Steel yourself, Special Agent Kelsey Hawk. I don't know if you are ready to hear about the Enchanted Highway."

Kelsey scoffed and shook her head. "I've seen things, Deputy. I've seen things that keep me awake at night. Let me have it."

Kelsey would have been on the edge of her seat if the seatbelt didn't tether her to the backrest. The weirdest things always happened in the smallest towns. There was more crime in the big cities, but she could understand how someone might go crazy out here with nothing but endless blankets of white.

"Do you have a strong stomach?" John asked with a smile. He was putting on a brave face, but the way he kept glancing to the side to look at the storm clouds as the road sleekly curved toward it showed his fear.

"Will you just lay it out for me," Kelsey said, becoming frustrated with him.

"Art, Special Agent Hawk. Art as far as the eye can see."

"What?" she asked.

"Depending on the day. Can we see thirty miles into the distance? Anyway, art for a thirty-mile stretch."

"Okay, you've lost me," Kelsey said.

"That's what the Enchanted Highway is. Gary Greff made a bunch of sculptures along the roadside. He's a local legend in this area. He made these giant metal sculptures of animals and dinosaurs and all types of things. They line the highway for about thirty miles. I don't know if it was to attract visitors, but they sure do the job. Once you get done with the City of Bridges, the Enchanted Highway is worth the drive. Maybe wait for better weather."

"That's it? The way you were acting back there, I thought you believed there was something unnatural about it."

"No, I'm not worried about that. We won't find him if we don't beat this storm out there. And if we get stuck in the storm, we're as good as dead. I know this area, and I trained in the military, but I'll die out here if we get stuck in the snow on the highway. This is a race against time."

Kelsey felt afraid for the first time in a long time. It was one thing to enter a building to take down evil but another to drive head-first into a storm. She could accept being shot in the line of duty, but not literally freezing her ass off on a highway in the middle of nowhere, enchanted or not.

"And a heads-up about the storm. If we do get a lightning storm with the snow, we might have power outages across town. We have a backup generator for the sheriff's office, but we will be dealing with that as well as the case."

"A power outage." Kelsey thought out loud. "When we get back to town, I want you to check if there were any power outages in the wider area over the days before you found the first body."

"What are you thinking?"

"I think he was prepared, but something out of his control happened. How common are power outages?"

"More common in the cold climate up here than down south."

"What if he was ready to kill her; maybe he stalked her for a while, but when he took her, there was a power outage. He loses all his freezing equipment. So, he turns to plan B. He takes the body to a place he knew had the equipment, so he could kill her there."

"So, he freezes them to death?"

"I don't know yet. The cold is part of it, but we won't know until we get the autopsy report. Check that for me, and I also want to widen the search for a van. We've been operating on the assumption that he's got a refrigerated vehicle to transfer the bodies, but Marcy said something on the phone about it being cold enough out that they didn't need a refrigerated truck to move the body to the lab. If he's transporting the bodies at night, he could use any truck, but it would have to be a decent size. He'll need equipment, too. Everything points to him working alone, and if that is the case, then he needs a way to move blocks of ice that weigh a ton. So, widen the search to include all trucks in the area, along with equipment like a small crane that could be rigged up, pulleys, jacks, forklifts, and things like that."

"That's a lot," John said.

"I know, but we need to find this guy. No one said it was going to be easy."

"There!" John shouted.

"Oh, wow," Kelsey replied. "They are kind of cool." She looked at the metal form of a giant chicken on the side of the road.

"No, the SUV," John corrected.

Kelsey looked farther up the highway to where a silver SUV was parked on the shoulder. No clouds of smoke came from the exhaust, and the windows were steamed up. She worried they would find another dead body; if he *was* the killer, they might never find closure. He would take all his secrets to the grave.

John pulled up behind the SUV, and they both tried to look in through the back window. The windows were not steamed up; they were iced up. Thunder rumbled almost directly above them, and Kelsey wanted to beg John to take them back to town.

That would show weakness.

Instead, she got out of the truck first to brave the cold and approach the vehicle. Kelsey went around the passenger side and bent down to try and see inside, but she couldn't make anything out. She couldn't even see how many people were in the car. John circled the car first before he put up both his hands to tell her to wait. He reached for the passenger door, and Kelsey quickly rounded it, her hand on her gun again.

She could see by the gentle nod of John's head that he was counting to five before opening the door. He pulled it open and jumped back immediately, reaching for his gun. Kelsey expected a dead body to fall out, but there was a blinding flash instead as a blade cut through the air toward John, just missing his stomach.

CHAPTER FOURTEEN

"Frank! What are you doing?" John screamed.

Kelsey flicked the clasp off her holster, but John held up his hands again and didn't reach for his gun.

"Don't come any closer!" Frank screamed from within the vehicle. "I'll cut you! I know what you want from me!"

Kelsey rounded the front of the vehicle to look in. She saw a man who was freezing to death. His teeth clicked together as he shivered, and he held a knife in his hand. The fingers curled around it were purple, and they looked rigid, as if he couldn't let go of the knife if he wanted to. When he saw Kelsey, he moved the knife back and forth in the air between them. His hair was covered in mini icicles—his eyelashes too.

"Frank, it's me. John, remember? You know who I am, Frank."

"Why have you come for me?" Frank shouted, but there was uncertainty in his voice now. He blinked constantly, the ice causing him discomfort.

"Dawn wanted us to check on you," John said.

Frank rubbed the side of his head with his free hand. "I think she's seeing someone else." His voice cracked.

"We just want to get you back to town, Frank. Dawn's worried about you." He spoke with a soothing voice as if he had dealt with this situation hundreds of times before.

"Who is it? Is it you?" His eyes turned wild again, and he shook the knife.

Kelsey was not worried about him lunging for them. He was waving the knife, but he was weak.

"Frank, come on. You know me. I wouldn't do something like that. Dawn wouldn't do something like that either. I know it feels hard at times, but look inside and ask yourself if Dawn would ever do anything to hurt you."

"They were coming for me," Frank hissed.

"Who was coming for you?"

"The animals. I couldn't leave the car, or they would get me. It was too far to walk."

"Okay, that's good, Frank. Where were you going to walk to?" John asked.

Kelsey was impressed by his negotiation techniques. Maybe John's talents were wasted in a small town. He spoke to Frank directly and with respect. He didn't talk down to him or make him feel bad about the situation. John was the voice of reason, and he was comforting.

"I was going to walk back to town. The car stalled, and I couldn't get it started. I couldn't leave, or the animals would get me. I was stuck. I'm stuck, John."

"Hey, we all get stuck at times, but listen to me. The storm is coming, and it's cold out here. I want to warm you up and get you back to Dawn, but you have to work with me. I want to get us back to safety. Can you work with me, Frank?"

Frank nodded and shivered.

"First, I want you to let go of the knife. Special Agent Hawk and I are here, and we have guns. We will fend off any animals if they come."

Frank looked toward Kelsey. She felt out of her depth in a situation like this but followed John's lead. "I passed the FBI-mandated shooting course with flying colors, Frank. I can hit a cougar from a hundred paces."

"Yeah, yeah, yeah, that's good," Frank managed.

"The knife, Frank," John reminded.

Kelsey glanced down at Frank's shoes, but he wore a regular black pair of sneakers. She held her breath while they waited for Frank to drop the knife. Eventually, there was a clank as the blade hit the asphalt below.

"That's great, Frank. I'm just going to take this knife and hand it to Special Agent Hawk. Then, I'm going to take you to my truck and take you back to town. We can have a tow truck come out and bring your car back, but we have to wait for the storm to pass."

Frank stared ahead and didn't say anything else. John picked up the knife and passed it to Kelsey. She took it in her gloved hand, holding the end of the handle. She quickly took it back to the truck and found an evidence bag.

She didn't like having Frank in the truck with them, but there was no other option.

John helped him onto the back bench and let him lie down without a seatbelt. The engine was still running, and the interior was warm. John turned up the heat and radioed back to town to let them know he was coming back with Frank and that Frank might need medical attention.

It reminded her a little of home. Not the endless snow outside or the maniac on the back bench, but the stifling heat of the car. Perhaps it was not the heat that was stifling but the case. Maybe they had the killer, or maybe they had someone who just needed help.

"Seen men turn like that plenty of times," John murmured. "It's always the heat or the cold. Almost got me once out in the desert, but my team was with me. I'm just glad I didn't have to disarm him. Had to do that before, too, but it's always better to choose the peaceful option when it presents itself. My family is my platoon now, and it doesn't do to be away from them when the storms roll in."

She stared at John as he drove. He was one of the good ones.

***

The storm rolled into town after the truck, and there was no hail as John had promised. There was no lighting either, just the low rumble of thunder. The power remained on, and that meant they could do their jobs as efficiently as possible with what they had.

"They say he's going to be in for a few days, maybe a week," John said. "He's got hypothermia, but his troubles go a lot deeper than that. I don't think his wife is cheating on him, but you never know. It doesn't concern the case."

"Does that mean…?" Kelsey asked from behind her desk.

"Yeah, he has an alibi too. He was with his wife all night. They had dinner, watched some TV, and went to bed at the same time. Even if he snuck out, I doubt he'd have time to go and collect a body and set it up in the middle of town."

"Could she be lying?" Kelsey asked. "Covering for him?"

"Yeah, it's possible, but I don't think so."

"So he's not our guy?"

"No, I don't think so. We're checking his house, just in case, and his wife is happy to comply with everything. He has many photos from Winter Fair, so there's a chance he caught on camera whoever did this if your theory about him coming back to view the spectacle is right."

"Talk to whoever is going through the photos, and I want pictures of anyone who was at Winter Fair who does not live in town. We know that the women frozen in the blocks of ice were not from the towns they were placed in, or they would have been identified immediately. He will not be from either of the towns either. I have a feeling that the women he chooses are on their own, too. I don't know if missing person reports will give us anything, but we keep going with them. Where are we with the shoes?"

John held up a sealed bag—the shoes contained within. "I went to Franks's house, and his wife let us search the place. They were in his front closet. I did a bit of detective work on the internet, and it turns out the shoes are not entirely uncommon. There are a few for sale on eBay. One of the big tech companies in Illinois ran a promotion a few years back where they gave away a pair of limited edition shoes with every laptop purchase. And by limited, I mean a hundred thousand pairs. Worked pretty well—they gave away all of them to customers except for some they gave to employees. It says TechNerd on the side in glow-in-the-dark letters."

"All right. I know it's a lot to add, but we need to find out who in the company got a pair and who bought a laptop around that time."

"Already ahead of you, boss," John smiled. "It will take some time, but I called in a few volunteer deputies, and they are checking with TechNerd. I've got them going through eBay and other online marketplaces for the resale market."

Kelsey smiled. She was impressed with his foresight.

"Good work, Deputy. There's hope for you yet." She regretted putting it like that when she was genuinely impressed by his work now and back at the vehicle.

"Okay, the killer doesn't know we know about the shoes, so we keep that on the down-low for now. I want to scour pictures of Winter Fair for anyone else wearing those shoes, and I want to check all the CCTV from our town and Westerly before we release this information to the public. I don't want to spook him and for him to get rid of the shoes."

She wasn't sure if the deputy had caught her slip. She had called it *our town*. Not even a week here, and she was thinking of it as home.

Have I lost all hope of getting out of this place?

John's phone rang, and he fished it out of his pocket. He held up the phone.

"It's the sheriff." John hit the button. "Hey, Sheriff."

63

He was silent for a long time as the sheriff spoke at the other end, but Kelsey could read on his face that there was another body. She felt like a failure.

"All right, we'll get there as soon as we can," John said before he hung up.

"Please say it's not another," Kelsey pleaded.

John sighed. "It's another."

"A third small town?"

"No, it's not like the other ones. I don't know if it was the extra police presence at the winter festivals or if this was even the same guy. It's the same thing—a body in a block of ice, but someone found it dumped on a frozen lake about forty miles north of here."

"Let's go," Kelsey said.

"Yeah, we will; we just need to be careful. It's a blizzard out there, but Sheriff Anderson is worried we won't make it in time."

"In time? What's going on?"

"They are having trouble getting out onto the lake to retrieve the body with the storm, and the ice is starting to crack. If it gets through, it will move toward the Chattanu River and get lost in the mountains. We can chase it, but chances are we won't be able to follow it down the valley with the storm and the amount of snow we've had. That means we might not retrieve the body until spring.

CHAPTER FIFTEEN

John slowed when a red and blue flashing light appeared in the distance.

"Oh, good," Kelsey said.

"We're not here yet. We're not even halfway."

"What then? An accident?"

"Cowherd Bridge is up ahead. They'll be closing access until they can clear it."

The snow battered the windscreen. The flakes were large, and no matter which way they turned, the snow was blown at them directly. The windshield wipers worked fine, but once the snow was wiped from the glass, they could only see a few feet before them.

John slowed to a stop as the uniformed officer with a flashlight and flag walked toward him. He was covered in a long yellow parka that was tight around his neck and reached down to his large boots. The hood was up and pulled tight, showing just his eyes.

"Deputy, there's no way through. They won't have it clear until the snow stops. No point until then."

"No worries," John said. "Hey, are you staying warm out here?"

"Oh, yeah," the officer replied. "You know how it is."

"Sure do. All right, we'll turn around and take the long way."

"The long way?" Kelsey fretted.

"Don't worry, I've been driving these roads since I was ten."

"Ten?" Kelsey asked.

"Only in a tractor," John replied as if that was sufficient explanation.

They turned in the opposite direction they had come, and the snow still blew toward them. Everything was white except for the gray sky above.

I'm going to die just like them. They will find the two of us encased in ice.

Frank Cobb had not been out in the elements for long, and it had been before the storm rolled in. He had almost died. If the truck stalled, they might be stranded miles from everywhere.

John turned off the highway into what looked like a field and plowed through the snow. There were no tracks up ahead. Kelsey gripped tight to the armrests. She thought of more and more ways they could die.

John drove faster than she would have, but he knew the area and was used to the roads. She could feel the wheels slide out from under them occasionally, but the deputy didn't lose control. Kelsey leaned forward in the passenger seat, trying to see something, but it was impossible. Everything looked the same. The beautiful pure white was also their curse. It took everything, the landscape, and landmarks, and removed them from the world.

Maybe that's what people do out here! They just drive anywhere there is snow and worry about the consequences later.

The chiming of her phone took her mind from the death she saw all around, and she whipped it out. It was an email from Marcy.

"Hey, they've identified the two bodies," Kelsey said.

"All right, who do we have?"

"Lisa Wainwright and Jessica Brown. Lisa is from Elkwater, and Jessica is from Ridley; they are in contact with the local police, but there were no missing person reports filed for either of them or from what they can discern so far, no immediate family."

No immediate family.

It sent a chill down Kelsey's spine. She felt an instant connection with the two women. She did not know who the woman was out on the lake, but she was sure she would have a similar story. It created more fear, but only that she would not catch him. She had to catch him if she was going to feel any peace.

"Hey, are you all right? You went all quiet, and you look like you've seen a ghost."

"Will you please watch the road," Kelsey snapped. "Sorry, I'm thinking about the women. Do you know either of them?"

"No, I don't, but I know the towns. This is going to rock them both for a long time. They're good people there, and they don't deserve this. No one deserves this."

"Could they be connected? The women?"

"Maybe; I don't know. I know some people from both towns, and I'll talk with them when we get back to Winchburgh. Does this feel like random killings to you?" John asked.

"It does, and it doesn't. I think he is choosing them randomly, but he's looking for a specific type of woman. He wants them to be found but doesn't want them to be missed. Maybe it's easier to target women he can take and—"

Kelsey didn't want to say it, but she worried he was taking these women and not killing them immediately. She didn't want to voice what he might be doing to them before he ended their lives.

To John's credit, he didn't vocally speculate either.

"We're almost there," John said after they had ridden silently through the snow.

Time ceased to exist in the blizzard; everything was the same in the white death. She felt herself becoming used to it. She would not want to drive through these conditions, but she was comfortable with John navigating the snow-covered prairies.

When she saw more flashing lights up ahead, she knew they had arrived—there were too many for it to be a barricade. John stopped the truck and told Kelsey to wait inside. He went to the back of the vehicle, and when he returned, he was wearing the same large jacket as the officer had worn when they turned around. He held another one and helped Kelsey into it when she stepped out of the truck. She zipped it up and pulled the drawstrings on the hood. The snow still stung her eyes, and even with the extra layers, the cold still nipped at her.

They trudged through the snow, looking for whoever was in charge.

"Deputy Gallant and Special Agent Hawk," John shouted through the swirling wind to a man with a bushy mustache.

"Reserve Deputy Wallace," he called back. "Boy, are we glad to have you both here. We've got a couple of the guys out on the ice with quads, but they're having right trouble getting the body back here."

"They saw it? There's definitely a body out there?" Kelsey asked.

"Oh, yeah, some kids were out on the lake before the storm rolled in and spotted it. We got here as soon as we could. I'm way out of my depth here, but if they can't get it back to safety soon, I'm not risking our men out there any longer."

"Be ready to extract them immediately," John said. "I won't lose any men out here today. Not to this."

"Do they have a camera?" Kelsey asked. "If they can't bring it in, they need to get photos of it."

"I'll talk to someone now."

"I don't care if it's just their phone camera. Any pictures are better than none," Kelsey said.

The reserve deputy got straight on the radio to call his men to do as Kelsey asked. She looked around as he spoke to them. She could not see the lake, and even if she could, she was sure he wouldn't know which part under the snow was lake and which wasn't.

"Why out here? Why dump it on a lake? I don't think that was an accident. If he couldn't put it on display for us in a town, he put it on display here for another reason." Kelsey looked around again. "He brought it here in his truck, but we have no chance of finding tire marks in this." Kelsey wiped the ice from her eyes. "He couldn't have planned the storm. This was another present for us." She was thinking out loud again. "He gives us gifts, and the ice is his wrapping."

"They got it!" someone shouted.

Kelsey placed a hand over her eyes, shielding them from the snow. It reminded her of the butcher's. The snow obscured everything, but a shadow appeared in the white, and that shadow materialized into two quads pulling a large block of ice. A chain was wrapped around the block, and it was lying down as they dragged it to safety.

She was lying down.

Kelsey could see the shape of a body inside, and she knew it would be a woman. She approached it quickly, hoping it would offer some kind of clue as to who had killed her. She wore a pink blouse and had ruby-red lipstick. The woman had a bright smile and wide eyes, but she still looked at peace.

"There are markings on the bottom," Kelsey said. She bent down. "Was that from the chain?" she shouted, indicating the large chunk missing from the end with the woman's feet.

"No, ma'am," the quad driver replied. "It was scuffed up like that when we got to it."

"I think he levered it out of his truck," Kelsey said to John. "Look, there are paint marks along the bottom of the block under her back. He stood the other two ice blocks on the stage, and he must have some sort of industrial lifting equipment, but this one was lying down. He used a crowbar or something to lever it out of his truck and onto the ice. Doing that with the weight was dangerous, but he thought it was worth the risk. He's meticulous, but he's unhinged too. As soon as we get this back to the lab, I want to know what vehicle the paint came from. I also want us to look again at the photos of the previous two victims when they were found. If we can find markings, we might have a clue as to what equipment he is using."

Kelsey didn't feel the cold anymore. She had a fire in her belly.

CHAPTER SIXTEEN

"Thank you all for being here," Kelsey said. "Sheriff Anderson has kindly agreed to direct all resources to the case for now, and I appreciate that."

Sheriff Anderson grimaced from the back of the room. She had not needed to ask him for the extra resources; he was out of his depth, and he had begrudgingly allowed Kelsey to take over. She looked out at the patrol officers and volunteer deputies. If she didn't take control of this case soon, they would send more FBI agents, and she would be kicked down the ladder. Perhaps SAC Granger had influenced the decision not to send anyone, or the storms slowed down any backup. For now, she was on her own.

"I want to thank you all for your work on this case so far. The best weapon we have against this guy is your local knowledge and connection with the local population. I'm not going to sugarcoat this: he's killed three women so far, and he will kill again. There seems to be no concrete connection between any of the women other than being loners. They were functioning members of society, but they didn't have any family, and they didn't have many friends. They kept to themselves. We don't know why he is targeting these women, but it points to him being a loner too. He won't have any immediate family around, nor will he have any close friends. He might be a functioning member of society but only on the outside."

The cause of death might give them something to go on, but they were still waiting on the autopsy reports.

Kelsey's cause of career death would be not catching this guy. If someone else caught him, her career was over; if no one caught him, her career was over. She needed to get him and get him fast, or Granger would be right. That would be the worst part.

And now, I'm here. I'm giving out orders when I've never been very good at following orders.

"We don't know where he lives, but we are sure he lives in the state. The women were taken within a four-hundred-mile radius of this point, likely putting him somewhere near Bismarck." Kelsey indicated the map on the wall behind her. "He will have a facility where he can deal with the bodies before moving them out, and he will have a residential address too. I don't think they will be in the same place. They will be close but separate.

"The first two bodies were put on display for us, but with the extra presence of police at the winter festivals, he had to adapt. The third body was placed on a lake. It was more rushed, but it was still deliberate. Marcy, what do you have for us?"

"Um, Stewart Lake is also known as the Lake of Life. People swim there in the summer, but there's a tradition to swim there just as the ice breaks at the start of spring. It's supposed to make you younger," Marcy said.

"Thank you, Marcy. This guy is local, and he has local knowledge. He wants transformation. He never fit in with society and wants change, maybe for himself or maybe for the women. There is some trauma in his past. The bodies are not a gift to us but a gift to the world. We are just the ones to find them."

"John, you spoke to some people who live close to the lake?" Kelsey asked.

"I did. There's ice fishing there over the winter, but they dismantled the tents with the storm coming in. A couple of days before the storm, they had a guy come down and ask them about ice fishing. He was nice enough, and they didn't think anything of it, but he was not local, so they remembered him. Unfortunately, he was covered from head to toe. The cold is a good disguise. Still, if this is our guy, then we know he's a guy. He didn't have an accent, was most likely Caucasian, and was around six feet tall. He matches what we caught on CCTV at Absolute Zero. No one spotted a vehicle."

"We are closing the net around this guy. I hate to say this, but he will kill again, and that is in our favor. If he were to lay low now, he might get away with it, but he would be out there looking for his next target. He doesn't make mistakes, but he does leave evidence. For now, I want all resources focused on the vehicle. Deputy?"

John stood up again. "We scraped the paint marks from the ice, and it is a color called *Frozen White*. This color is only used by Ford, so we know what he was driving when he moved the body onto the ice. I want all records of Ford vans and trucks in the area in Frozen White."

"This would have been a big truck, most likely a Ford Transit," Kelsey said. "It needs a large load capacity, and it's more likely a van than a truck so he can better conceal the bodies and the equipment needed to transfer them to the stages, in the case of the first two. I want you to liaise with Deputy Gallant on any vehicles found, and we will slowly check on each of them. Keep your eyes and ears open, and thank you again."

The small team was dismissed, and everyone went straight to work. Kelsey was glad to be back in the confines of the sheriff's office, with the storm still raging outside. Once the majority were gone, she looked at John and shook her head. He sighed and shrugged.

"How long have you been awake?" John asked.

"Too long," Kelsey replied. "There's not much we can do right now, so I'm going to head back to my place, get a pizza, and sleep as long as possible. I'll leave my phone on in case you find anything."

"Okay," John said.

Sheriff Anderson approached once everyone had left the room. "Special Agent Hawk, you might be leading this investigation, but I am still in charge here. Everything runs through me, and I mean everything. We run a tight ship and are darn good at it when we do."

"Yet, you don't have the first clue about what to do next, do you?" Kelsey asked, all her resentment toward her former SAC flooding back.

"Excuse me!" The sheriff's face reddened, and he balled his fists.

"You heard me, Sheriff. I don't care what issues we have between us. I don't care who's in charge. All I care about is getting this guy. I'm not going to stand in your way, and I hope you won't stand in mine. Can we at least agree on that?"

Sheriff Anderson stood in front of Kelsey, but much like with the case, he didn't know what to do next. The only thing he could do to save face was turn and storm out.

Kelsey shook her head at his receding form.

"Wait until you catch him at The Old Mill Tavern on a Friday night," John joked. "Plays that same darn song on the jukebox about a dozen times when he's drunk. He doesn't have any kids, but he still loves Taylor Swift. He gave me this earlier to pass on to you."

Kelsey opened the folder handed to her and scanned the files within.

"Cause of death?" John asked.

"The cold," Kelsey replied. "They literally froze to death. I don't know much about causes of death, but I imagine it would have been painless. It might have been slow, but the body would have shut down."

"Does that fit with everything so far?" John asked.

"Yeah, I think it does, and so does what he did to them after death."

John frowned, and he mimicked the sheriff momentarily. Still, it was not something she could shelter him from.

"The autopsy report from the first two murders show that they were *posed* post-mortem, or after they were frozen—whichever came first. He killed them, and before they were frozen solid, he posed them: a scream, peaceful sleep, and a smile. He transformed them once they were dead."

CHAPTER SEVENTEEN

Kelsey woke with a start, but she knew she was not really awake; she was not in control of her body either. She was in her bedroom, just as she remembered it: the pale wallpaper, the cracks in the ceiling, the old smell imbued in the house, and the scratchy blanket that irritated her until she fell asleep. Then it hugged her and kept her warm and safe until morning. But not tonight.

She lay in her bed with the blankets pulled up to her neck. As long as she was under the blankets, she was safe.

A soft thud jolted her again. She had to investigate the noise just as her parents would. She held her breath to listen for another sound in the house—complete silence. She pulled back the blankets and shuffled to the edge of the bed so it would not creak as she got out. She stepped onto the carpeted floor and moved silently to the door.

She listened again—nothing.

Kelsey steeled herself and moved from the room, sticking to the wall as she made her way down the corridor lit by the dull nightlight plugged into the wall near the floor. She moved opposite the light so she would not cast shadows that would be seen by whatever entity had invaded their house.

A movement caught her eye, and Kelsey looked to the right, staring into eyes she hadn't seen for twenty years. She looked at the young girl, her own childish features, and begged her not to continue—if she didn't see it, it might not have happened.

She was not in control of her younger self, and the small girl held the mirrored gaze for a moment more before she looked away and walked down the hallway to where her younger sister slept. She moved down the hallway carefully until she was at her sister's door. She looked in.

Kelsey held her breath to stop from making a noise. Her eyes widened at her sister's still form. The bedspread was new—white with a large burgundy floral design in the middle, glistening in the pale moonlight streaming through the open window. The flower blossomed before her eyes.

73

She moved out of the room, not looking behind into the hallway. She backed up, staring at her sister's bed until she got to her parents' room. The curtains were open a sliver, and a silver stripe cut across the bed, cutting the matching burgundy flowers on her parent's bedspread—one for her mother and one for her father. It was too dark to see, but she felt the flowers blossom in the darkness. With new life came death.

The curtain fluttered, and the pale silver blade danced around the room. Another noise: the careful shuffle of feet on carpet. Her heart turned to ice; her veins tightened. She did not look behind. Her feet took her to the closet at the room's far end. She slipped inside and pressed her nose to the slats to peer out. She could only see the bed, the lifeless lumps that once were her family. She did not make a sound.

The final sound: a creak from downstairs. It could have come from anything, but she knew they were gone—she saw the door open and close in her mind. She could not leave the closet—not now, not ever. She remained there until a shadow crossed it, and the door was flung open. She looked up into her eyes and screamed.

Kelsey gasped as she sat bolt upright in bed. The scream caught in her throat—reality was as quiet as her dream; the cold sweat on her forehead was as icy as the outside temperature. She could let go of some of the pain if she let it out, but she didn't want to. She wanted to stuff it deep down inside to be used later. She had managed with it for twenty years and would keep it simmering in her soul forever if needed.

She wiped her brow with the back of her hand and pulled off the blankets. She did not move for a moment, listening in the darkness for any sounds in the small apartment. It was warm in the bedroom, but her bones were cold. She turned her head to the side, but there was nothing—the entire town was silent. Kelsey clicked on the lamp on the bedside table and closed her eyes against the invading light.

She might consider this her town after briefly being here, but she did not consider the room or apartment to be home. She glanced around at the familiar but foreign furniture, checking the shadows to make sure none were new and there was no movement. She rubbed her eyes again before she swung her legs over the side of the bed. She pulled open the drawer on the bedside table and pulled out the folder.

Nothing was written on the front; all it contained was one newspaper clipping. Even though she knew the article by heart, she still opened the folder and read the headline.

Child Orphaned as Three Killed in Home Invasion

Kelsey felt no emotion as she read through it. She knew the article was about her parents and sister, but it said nothing about them other than how they were killed. The writer didn't know her family; it might as well have been any other people. It was in her dreams where the emotion came flooding back—where the little girl felt fear, but her grown self could only channel remorse as she inhabited the small girl repeatedly and still couldn't save them.

If she had woken earlier, she might have been able to do something, anything. Or the killer would have murdered her too, stabbed her in the chest just like her parents and sister, and her own scarlet flower would have bloomed on her bedcovers. She could have joined them in rest instead of having to live her life without them, vowing to avenge them but never getting any closer to the truth.

Why? Why was I left alive?

Why was she left alive? Why did someone enter their home? Why was her family killed? Was it only one person? Did they leave her alive on purpose?

Twenty years and more questions than answers. When there were zero answers, it was easy to have more questions.

Kelsey didn't feel like an orphan anymore—it was hard to feel like an orphan when you were thirty years old. Growing up in the foster system had toughened Kelsey, and the morals and values that her parents instilled had stuck with her. Her father was a cop, and her mother was a coroner; it was no wonder she had taken this path in life. The only surprising thing was the destination.

When she tackled a case, she always wondered what her father would make of the evidence or what her mother would discover about a body. What would they have thought about their own murders? Three stab wounds, all through the heart, leaving three dead bodies. Nothing was taken from the house. No forced entry. Was it supposed to happen like that? Was it a home invasion, or was it something more?

And what about the current case? Would her mother or father have anything to say about it that Kelsey hadn't already thought about? Would they see the case any differently?

Always so many questions and not enough answers. She would never know their opinion on anything ever again. There would always be three voids in her life.

Kelsey put the article away and got out of bed. It was late or early, depending on how you looked at it—either way, she could not sleep. She walked to the window and opened the curtain. It was dark, but the blanket of snow illuminated the town, reflecting the moonlight. Snow fell lazily, creating a thin, fresh coat. She could feel the chill from the glass.

They had nothing on her family's killer or killers, but Kelsey knew they would kill again if they had not already. No one does that to three people and retires from a murderous life. There were no leads, and she was confident there never would be. Still, she grasped tightly to the thought that crashed around her mind late at night.

Once a killer, always a killer.

That was the best plan of action she had. If she did not know who killed her parents, then catch killers one by one until they were all caught. Maybe the killer was dead, maybe they were old now, or maybe they were out there killing still. If she did this long enough, she might catch the person who had brutally murdered her family.

She might never know she had caught them, but the thought kept her going—pushed her to do whatever was needed to get justice.

Kelsey's eyes opened wide. Maybe there was another way to find this guy. She practically ran for the door after throwing on a few more layers before flying down the stairs and exiting back out into the bitter cold.

CHAPTER EIGHTEEN

A fresh layer of snow meant the roads had become treacherous, so he slowed the vehicle, carefully navigating the roads he had driven hundreds of times. It was one of the many things his father had instilled in him before he passed—no matter how much you know something, always do it thoroughly and do it right. He might have driven these roads numerous times and dealt with worse conditions, but over-confidence got you into trouble. Professional drivers crashed all the time, and they were better trained than anyone. He was confident he would reach his destination but did not switch off or move into autopilot. He watched the road as if his life depended on it.

And he did not want the hassle of having to call a tow truck if he spun off the road and into the ditch. His truck had four-wheel drive, but that was a safety net that was not worth testing. The best safety net was the one that never needed to be used.

"Beautiful, isn't it?" he asked as they continued down the long and winding road.

He chuckled to himself. He had not thought of the song in a long time, but it came flooding back to him like a crashing waterfall. He sang along in his head. He might have sung out loud if he could hold a tune. Another thing that had been instilled in him was knowing your limits. It was great to have ambitions and dreams, but they should live within your parameters. He knew he could not sing, so he would never try to pursue a career in singing, no matter how much he dreamed of it. He didn't dream of it at all, of course—he was merely illustrating the point to himself. Be careful and deliberate in everything you do, and act within your limitations, and you will be fine.

The radio crackled back into life as he neared the small town. Even though the drive was familiar, he was always intoxicated by the beauty of the town as it reared into view. The large wooden bridge stood magnificent, stained rich walnut against the white snow. Sometimes, the ice river beneath would reflect the bridge, but a light dusting of snow had removed the mirror. Still, it wasn't any less impressive.

There was something about bridges that had stuck in his mind since childhood. He had explored his fascination with them but had never been able to pinpoint where the love had come from. He would never employ a therapist to explore it—those hacks were not worth the money. There was a transitional aspect to them—the crossing of a boundary. A river, even a small one, meant death in winter. You might cross it, but it would cut you to the bone, dragging the life from you even as you walked away. Yet, a simple bridge guarded against death. Cross over a bridge, and you were safe; go under, and you better be careful.

They were a testament to humankind, a subtle reminder that obstacles could be conquered.

A Bridge Over Troubled Waters.

The song replaced the previous one, and he hummed along as he waited for the radio channel to stop crackling so he could turn it up. He had once thought about theater, but he was tone-deaf, and they said he couldn't act either. It was enough to quell his dream, but there were other ways to perform. That was his third lesson. Always be ready to adapt. Life will not always go your way, nor should you expect it to.

"Please." The begging voice from the backseat of the truck was muffled.

The song quickly left his mind, and he sighed heavily. He was not annoyed with her, just disappointed she couldn't follow his simple instructions. He had high hopes that she would be the smartest of them all and would do as she was told, but she was just like the rest.

He flicked the lever under the steering wheel to indicate he was stopping on the side of the road even though there were no other cars out. He pulled over safely and turned off the lights—the two of them sat silently for a while. He wanted to make sure she was done talking before he doled out the punishment. When he was satisfied, he opened the driver's door and got out. He checked the surrounding area—better to be safe than sorry—and then opened the rear passenger door on the side facing the ditch.

He pulled her from the vehicle, being firm but fair. He did not need to hurt her, but she had to be taught a lesson. The woman wore leggings under a long silver skirt and a puffy black jacket. He had removed her gloves so she could be bound at the wrists and carefully placed them in her coat pockets. She was wearing a wool hat, but he took it off, releasing her long, black, curly hair. He forced her down to her knees in the snow. He waited again to hear her say something more through the gag in her mouth. She was quiet this time.

"Good," he said.

He went to the back of the truck and unlocked the cover. He pulled the large container of water to the edge of the truck bed and placed a smaller container under the tap. He dosed out exactly one liter of water.

"My grandmother never measured, of course," he said to her. "She would often use the hose, and you can't measure the amount from a hose. When she couldn't reach us with the hose, she would use a cup or jug or whatever else was on hand. Always cold water—freezing water from outside. She would plunge the vessel through the ice and into the water below and then throw it at us."

He tossed the water onto the woman. She gasped through the gag at how cold it was. The water had been sitting in the truck's bed for hours, and he didn't need to test it to know it was almost ice cold. The woman recoiled from the water and looked up at him with pleading eyes.

"Please," she uttered again through the thick cloth.

The man sighed. "When I measure it, it makes sense. It's funny how negatives can be turned into a positive, isn't it?" He returned to his truck with the empty container and refilled it. "You won't think this is helping you, but it is. I was like you once, but the world must have order. Her methods were unorthodox, but they hardened me against the world—they brought order to my life. Do you think I steal cookies from the jar anymore? Figuratively speaking, of course."

He smiled when she did not answer him. She was learning but still had to be punished for her outburst. He tossed the water into her face, drenching her thick curls. Steam rose from her as she started to shiver. She looked him in the eye and pleaded with her gaze, but she did not vocalize it this time.

"I will bring order to your life, too," he said. "Don't worry; the others acted out. Some learned, and some did not. I promise there will be no pain as long as you do as I say. Do you need more water?"

She shook her head, shivering the entire time.

"And are you going to be quiet?"

She shook as she nodded.

"I always found deep meaning in the silence." The man smiled. "When you close out the outside noise, you can listen to your thoughts. Listen to what you are telling yourself. Soon, you will have the greatest silence of all. I envy you, Rebecca. I can help people to get there, but I won't have my own silence for a long, long time."

Rebecca looked down at the snow beneath her. The water had worked exactly as intended, exactly as it had worked on him when he was four. She would not have time to understand how much he had helped her, but he hoped she trusted his wisdom. He had not learned to trust his grandmother until she was gone.

He hated her more than anyone he had ever known but understood her ways. It had all been for his own good.

Now, he could free others.

CHAPTER NINETEEN

"Morning," John said through a half-stifled yawn. He walked into the office carrying two cups of coffee and set one down on Kelsey's desk beside two more cups of coffee.

"Morning," Kelsey replied, picking up one of the coffees she had brought in and handing it to John. "I guess we get two cups of coffee each this morning."

"That's fine by me," John replied.

He walked over to the empty desk in the small makeshift FBI office. Since they had been working the case together, he had all but moved into the FBI office with Kelsey, taking Special Agent Wood's desk while he was in Bismarck.

"I couldn't sleep last night. I pretty much chugged this one on the way in," he held the almost-empty cup aloft, "so I'm ready to get started on cup number two."

"You had bad dreams too."

Kelsey bit her bottom lip. She had no idea why she had said it. Perhaps it was the fact he had brought her coffee while her old boss, the boss who was still intent on making her life hell, had only brought problems. Deputy Gallant wasn't her boss—she was technically his—but she was new, and he was not, so she was fine deferring to him sometimes. Maybe it was because he was nice to her and respected her without feeling threatened. Maybe it was a million things.

"You had bad dreams?" John asked.

"I thought I could look for any shops in the wider area that might have repainted his truck, but I've come up with nothing so far. I should have stayed in bed. How are we doing with the search for the truck?" Kelsey asked, changing the subject. She had no intention of discussing her demons with a man she hardly knew. Not when a killer was on the loose, and every lead they followed led to a dead end.

Here's hoping we can follow a white Ford truck and find the bastard!

"That's what kept me up," John said. "Do you have any idea how many white Ford trucks there are in the area? And that's before we

81

even reach bigger cities like Bismarck and Fargo. I don't know how far we want to look, but if this guy is as smart as you say he is, he won't leave us an easy trail of evidence, will he?"

"Not intentionally," Kelsey responded. "I'm confident he will have covered his tracks as well as he can, but he only has what he thinks we are looking for to go on. There's no connection with the women; they were all taken from different places, all worked different jobs, were posed differently, and left in different places. Sure, his M.O. is the same in how he kills them, but I'm almost certain that will come down to psychological profile rather than any hard evidence we can trace. How is Marcy doing with the mental health centers?"

"Well, there are many more mental health problems in the state than there are white Ford trucks. Do you know the phrase a needle in a haystack? Well, imagine a million barns, each with a hundred haystacks, and we are not even sure we're looking for a needle."

"Mmm, your analogies could use a little work," Kelsey said.

John chuckled. "Yeah, we don't have the big-city analogies here in our small town, so you're going to have to deal with it, but we do have supportive deputies who will listen to anyone who wants to share their bad dreams. What was it? A clown? A monster under the bed?"

"Yeah, something like that," she replied. Her tone of voice told him not to probe any further. "Everything is a dead end. What's the betting that this guy has mental health problems but has never been diagnosed?"

"For all our sakes, I hope you're wrong, but I'm learning that you are not wrong about much."

"Hey, I try," Kelsey said, happy that she had avoided discussing what happened to her family. "Listen, I know it's going to be a long list, but we have to check them out individually. Before that, I need you to check the list of owners and see if there is anyone we should talk to first—anyone who stands out and might know something. Our killer is smart, and he's not going to be driving around in his own truck, so we look at people who have had a truck stolen. Or people who have had a truck stolen but haven't reported it. Is there someone who might sell him the truck for cash or be blackmailed into giving up their truck? That sort of thing. And I need it now because I'm getting sick of sitting in this office and doing nothing."

"You're not—"

Kelsey held up her hand. "I am. I'm going through files looking for a ghost; he might already have his next victim. He had to dump the last one because he couldn't display it like the others, which means two things: he will take another girl quickly because he shows no signs of slowing down, and he will be angry at us for ruining his plans. I'm sure he will adapt with no problem, but he will put on a show with this next one. So, I want to get out of here and catch this guy, and I want to do it before he kills again."

John didn't respond—he dove back into the files without hesitation. Kelsey went back to her work. She knew it was valuable, but it felt slow and tedious, and the longer it went on, the more risks she would be willing to take to nail the son of a bitch.

She took her mind off her frustration with the second coffee of the morning. It didn't feel like morning anymore after being in since well before dawn.

"What does the transformation mean?" John asked.

"What's that?"

"You mentioned transformation at the lake. That's why he poses them. This sort of stuff doesn't happen around here, so I am well out of my depth. When bad stuff happens in these parts, we look into it, and there is usually a mundane reason. A tractor has a part missing? Heck, let's check the next farm over, and chances are someone needed it to fix their tractor but couldn't afford it. Something gets stolen? Someone else probably needed some money. Someone is targeted? We look at the person who holds a grudge against them. Nine times out of ten, it's simple. This is different, isn't it?"

"He transforms them because he wants to transform himself," Kelsey said. "I'm not an expert in profiling, but that's my hunch. He's been through some trauma and needs to change, but he can't. It eats him up inside, but he can control it by controlling others. The poses, the ice, the locations; they all have something to do with him, and nine times out of ten, it's related to childhood."

Her dream came flooding back at the mention of childhood. Who was she to talk about childhood trauma and how it affected people when she was as messed up as she was and wouldn't do anything about it except put her life in constant danger? She would push for everyone but her to get help. Deep down, she knew she needed help, but she would never admit that.

"I don't understand it, but we're going to catch him all the same. You do your psychic voodoo stuff, and I'll do my hokey small-town stuff, and we'll meet somewhere in the middle," John said.

"That sounds like a plan," Kelsey replied.

That was something new too. Back in the city, everyone worked as a team, but everyone was also out to prove themselves—and Kelsey was the guiltiest. Yet, she wouldn't be surprised if John didn't care that she got all the credit when they solved this case. He reminded her a little of her father. When he was a cop, people were out to get the bad guys. Now, there was a lot more to do it. Perhaps it was the fact that she was a woman—she had to work harder to prove herself. Maybe it was—

"I might have something." John interrupted her thoughts.

"What is it?"

John got up from his desk with a printed document. "Would be surprised if he's our guy because he's usually sloppy as heck, but we should talk to him. I did as you said and went through all the trucks in the area, narrowing them down by the color, of course, and still checking for any that have been repainted, but I narrowed by capacity too, and if he was on the lake, then he's going to need four-wheel drive. Still a heck-ton of vehicles, but this one sticks out. Randy Frogg. His real name, unfortunately."

"He's known locally to law enforcement?" Kelsey asked.

"I don't think there's a cop in the area who hasn't had a run-in with Randy. He's a complete asshole, and he might be small-time, but he's unpredictable too. He would be into more serious stuff, given the chance, but more serious stuff doesn't happen around here. Except...."

"Let's go pay Randy a visit." Kelsey was already on her feet.

CHAPTER TWENTY

John parked the truck but kept the engine running so the heat would continue to run. They stared at the building in front. It looked like part diner, part bar, part gas station, and part souvenir store. It was dilapidated, but that didn't stop it from being full, evidenced by the noise and vehicles parked out front. The sign out front said *Reggie's* in big neon letters, but the second 'g' was out, not that it changed the name. The metal entrance had a small round glass window near the top, like a porthole on a ship.

Is that so you know what to expect before you go in?

There were three bikers standing, smoking by the door. It wasn't hard to tell they were bikers with how they were dressed; though, with the sheer number of motorbikes parked outside the building, it was a good bet that everyone inside was a biker.

"Local biker hangout?" Kelsey asked.

"Yeah," John said resignedly. He was watching the three bikers at the door.

Kelsey didn't need to ask. This place was trouble for most people, and John didn't want them to face the obstacle of having to get into the bar.

"It's a different world in there," John added. "The rules that apply to everyone don't apply to them. I know what you're going to say, but that's just the way it is, and it works for the most part. We don't police them unless we need to, and they do a pretty good job of policing themselves internally. We might have rival gangs trying to invade their territory from time to time, but for the most part, they stop a lot of crime."

"You let them break the law so others don't?" Kelsey asked.

"Things are different out here, and—"

"I get it," Kelsey said. "We have the same kind of thing in the city. Not gangs of bikers, but you have to let some things slip to maintain the status quo, right? If it works, it works. But what does it mean for us?"

85

"It means we talk to Randy here or wait until he goes home, and he's a hard man to catch at home. This is pretty much his office. It's not ideal, but if we want to move quickly, this is our best shot."

Kelsey shrugged. "I've gone into worse."

John snorted and shook his head. "Yeah, so have I. If you really want to compare horror stories, you only have to say."

Kelsey could feel something in the air between them—she might have her own horror stories, but she didn't want to hear John's. She watched the three men at the door—all large, with beards and thick forearms. They wore matching denim vests over their shirts, and none seemed to be affected by the cold. Their faces were weather-beaten and tanned from years of riding, and they sported wrinkles through age. It was not a place Kelsey wanted to venture into, especially when it was only the two of them.

Yet, she couldn't help but feel excited. The dream, the third body, the killer still out there—it drove her to take action. Her old boss was still after her too. She needed to take control of the situation and could only do so if there was something to take control of. It was the waiting that killed her. They might be walking into a shitshow, but it was one she could handle. It was a need she had to satisfy.

"Are we going to do this?" Kelsey asked when the three men at the door went back inside.

"Just follow my lead, and I don't want you to think I'm here to protect you, but if you get hurt, the sheriff will never let me hear the end of it. We should have run this by him and got permission first."

"Well, we don't have time for that, and I outrank him, so let me deal with that."

"Oh, I will, but you don't want to burn all your bridges in your first month here. Piss off the sheriff, and you might as well piss off the whole town."

Kelsey was reckless, but she wasn't stupid. The deputy was right—she had to act, but she needed to be careful. She had to control herself before she controlled a situation.

"Tell me what to do, and I'll follow your lead," Kelsey said.

John nodded and got out of the truck. Kelsey followed, and they headed for the bar together.

"Let me speak to them first. They might not like me, but they know me. Any chance I can convince you to stay outside?"

"Nope," Kelsey replied.

"In that case, try not to look anyone in the eye and keep your head down. There will be some women in there, but they don't look like you."

"I think that's a compliment," Kelsey said as they entered.

It was about as dark as Kelsey expected. There were no windows except for the small porthole in the front door. Neon signs dotted the back of the bar, and motorcycle memorabilia decorated the walls and ceiling. The boots lining three walls had seen better days, and it was hard to tell if the original color was black or a dirty red, and the tables and chairs in the center of the room were literally on their last legs. The bar was about half-full, and around half of the patrons watched them as they crossed the sticky floor from one side to the other.

"Deputy," a large man in a far booth called.

"Ernest," John called back.

"Need a seat, lass?" a biker called to Kelsey.

She didn't turn to face him and kept her mouth clamped shut. She had a dozen retorts locked and loaded, but this was not why they had come.

"What can we do for you, Deputy?" Ernest asked.

He was a little older than the other bikers. He was a big guy, and his fists looked like large slabs of meat—they were about as butchered as steaks; the man liked a fight, and Kelsey was sure he did well when he had to prove himself.

"We'd like a word with Randy," John said. He held himself tensely, ready to spring into action if needed.

One of the bikers in the booth behind Ernest's perked up. Kelsey knew that it was him without having to be introduced. He was a big guy too—everyone in the bar was big—but he looked more ferrety than the others. She didn't like to make needless assumptions, but he looked like a criminal.

"Go ahead," Ernest said.

"We'd prefer if he came down to the station with us," John said with a sardonic smile.

"Not sure I'd prefer that," Randy said without looking at either of them.

"So, there you go," Ernest said. "Unless you are here to arrest the lad, maybe you can let us all know why you are in here, Deputy. And bringing an FBI agent with you? I didn't know we were causing so much trouble."

Low laughter rippled around the bar. Kelsey didn't like any of these men and women, but she was a little impressed that he knew who she was. Word got around in a small town like this, but it was impressive, nonetheless.

Ernest stood up, and John's hand moved toward his belt.

"We're not going to have any trouble here, are we, Deputy?" Ernest asked.

Randy smiled from behind him, which annoyed Kelsey more than anything else so far.

The anger bubbled beneath John's cool, calm exterior, and a vein swelled on his neck. It was not a position she often found herself in, but Kelsey took it upon herself to try and de-escalate the situation. John had stated he would take the lead, and she had enough respect for him that she didn't want to go against that, but she was worried he would do something he would regret.

Better for me to make enemies than the deputy.

"Yeah, you bet your ass you're going to have trouble here," Kelsey stated. That gained the attention of the entire bar. "I presume you've heard about the three women who've been found?" By the silence they had. "I don't care what the fuck you do around here, but I don't want another innocent person murdered on my watch, and I'm sure you don't either. Do any of you have daughters?" More silence. "He doesn't target a certain type of woman. He could come for anyone. So, either you let us talk to Randy, or I'll make it my business to create some trouble around here, and if someone else is murdered," she stepped closer to Ernest, "I'm going to be extremely pissed off at you."

Ernest held her gaze, and she readied herself to grab her gun. He breathed out through his nose before he gestured with his head toward Randy. He sat back down and took a large swig of his beer, his mustache wet when he was done.

"Still my fucking choice what I do," Randy said as he finally stood to face them, "and no bitch gets to come in here and tell me what to do." He walked straight for Kelsey. "You might have a fancy badge, but around here—"

Randy didn't have a chance to finish as he stormed toward Kelsey. She raised her hand and slammed the 'v' between her thumb and forefinger into his neck. He choked on his words and fell to his knees, clutching his throat. A couple of the guys around the room started to laugh, and there were a couple of cheers.

"Cuff him," Kelsey said to John. "We can take him down to the station. He seems much more compliant after our little chat."

CHAPTER TWENTY ONE

Randy struggled in the truck's back seat, and he managed to push himself far enough forward to head-butt the back of the passenger seat. Kelsey felt her seat shake, but it was not enough to irritate her. She had dealt with guys like him before, and the best thing to do was to remain calm and ignore most of what they said.

"Hey, bitch! Are you listening to me, bitch! I'm going to kill you when I get out of here."

Randy had his hands cuffed behind his back and was wearing a seatbelt. He could struggle against it to get leverage to head-butt the back of her seat, but he couldn't get free. He might be able to get free if he thought it through, but he was too angry after being taken down in front of everyone in the bar, and now that he had his voice back, he had to do something about it. That something was mostly hurling insults toward Kelsey.

"Hey! You listening to me, bitch!"

"Shut the hell up!" John ordered. He craned his neck and turned around to face Randy even though he was driving. "Another word out of you, and I'll get the sheriff to bring a car down here to take you down to the station. We asked you to come with us, and you caused a scene. You don't know Special Agent Hawk very well, but she was being nice back in the bar. You don't want to get on the wrong side of her."

Kelsey wasn't sure if he was making it up to scare the guy or if he believed it about her.

"You do know we are looking for a killer, don't you?" Kelsey asked. "We can get you a lawyer if you like, but I can advise you not to make death threats to a woman when someone has already killed three women."

That shut him up briefly. They traveled around thirty seconds before he piped up again.

"I know my rights," he said. "I don't want to talk to anyone before I talk to my lawyer."

"Hey, Randy, you're not in any trouble," John said. "Yet! You're not under arrest, but that can change very quickly. All we want to do is ask you a few questions, but I need you to be calm before that, all right?"

There was silence from the back seat, and Kelsey couldn't tell if he was heeding the deputy's words or if he was being stubborn. Either way, it was nice not to have any noise.

"Where did you learn how to do that?" John asked. "The whole throat thing?"

"At the academy and a couple of times out in the field. Once in a bar when a guy grabbed my ass and wouldn't let go."

"He might have grabbed your ass," Randy said, "but you can suck on my—"

"All right!" John shouted. "Finish that sentence, and I *will* arrest you, Randy. Now, shut your darn mouth."

More silence from the back, but it was brimming with tension.

In the moment before Kelsey had slammed her fist into Randy's neck, she had looked him in the eye and knew he was capable of vicious things. Was he capable of three murders? He was an idiot, but that didn't mean he couldn't have killed. They had seen patterns before when they were not there. What if there was no pattern here, no root cause, no nothing? Could he have done this and left no evidence? She thought him capable of killing, but three people? It was a stretch.

Though he obviously has problems with strong women. He could have gone for John, but he came for me.

And he found out what happened to the people who came after her.

"What have you been up to these past few weeks, Randy?" John asked as he drove.

"Got bitches of my own to take care of," he replied.

Kelsey could practically hear his smirk.

"The less helpful you are, the angrier we are going to get, Randy. I can already have you arrested for attacking an FBI agent, and I'm sure if I ask around, I can find a dozen other crimes to attribute to you, so it's in your best interest to cooperate."

"I didn't lay a finger on her. I'll sue for assault."

"It's not how I say it," John replied. "You laid hands on her, and she acted in self-defense. Besides, Randy, do you really want everyone to know that you got your ass handed to you by a woman?"

Randy head-butted the passenger seat again, but he didn't hurl abuse with it this time.

"Stop messing around, Randy," John shouted. "Three women are dead! Three women! And they've not seen you around the bar lately. That's your hangout, but you haven't been hanging out there as regularly. So, if you don't tell us what you've been doing, we are going to have to speculate, and we really don't want to go down that road."

There was more silence from the back seat but a different silence now. John pulled into the sheriff's office and parked the truck. He turned off the heat this time but didn't get out. Both he and Kelsey turned to face Randy. He looked at Kelsey but bit his tongue. She had no doubt he would lunge for her if he weren't handcuffed and buckled into his seat. She could take care of herself in most situations, but fighting off an attacker in a cramped vehicle was a different story.

"I'll talk to you only,' Randy said to John. "Not the bitch."

"You *will* talk to me," Kelsey said. "This *bitch* is currently the only thing standing between you and this situation escalating. I say the word, and we ship you out of town. You might think you are a big deal here, but you're nothing compared to the monsters they'll lock you up with. Now, if you are intent on sabotaging my case, I have to believe there is a reason for that, and if you don't want to help us catch the killer, then what are you hiding?"

Randy looked at John.

"Don't look at me," John said. "You keep on with comments like that directed at the lady, and I will put you down."

Kelsey wasn't sure she had ever been called a lady before.

"I didn't kill no one," Randy said.

"That's a good start, Randy, but you had better start convincing me. If I took every criminal at their word, I wouldn't be in this job anymore. Where have you been for the last couple of weeks?" Kelsey asked.

"Yeah, all right, I haven't been in the bar as much, but I didn't kill anyone. I've been out doing stuff."

"Illegal stuff?" Kelsey asked.

"I... yeah."

"Good. Listen, Randy, I don't care about any of the shit you've been up to, all right? When we take you inside, I want you to tell us about what you've been up to and who might be able to corroborate that. If you can prove to me you didn't kill anyone over the past two weeks, you'll be free to go. Mess around again, and I will make it my mission to make your life hell. Do you understand me?"

Randy shook his head and looked away.

"I'll take that as a yes," Kelsey said. "Now, do you own a white Ford truck?"

Randy looked back at Kelsey quickly, and hesitation crossed his face. He looked to the side again as he contemplated what he was going to say.

Kelsey hated being made to wait, but she had come to an understanding with Randy, and he was speaking to her. Push him too much, and he would shut down out of stubbornness. Give him too much freedom, and he would try to weave a story.

Everyone was different—colleagues, criminals, killers. You just had to know what they were thinking, and you could get what you needed.

"The truck," Kelsey reminded.

"Yeah, I have a white truck."

"Would you happen to know if the color is Frozen White?" John asked.

"I don't know. I know it's white." Randy said.

"And is it parked at your house, Randy?" Kelsey asked.

"It... it *was*," Randy said.

"What do you mean *it was*?" John asked.

"It was stolen two months ago," Randy said.

"Bullshit!" John said. "Cut the crap, Randy. Where is the truck?"

Randy wriggled uncomfortably in his seat. "It was stolen, I swear to you. I was in the bar late one night, and when I went out, some prick was driving away in my truck."

"You expect us to believe that?" John asked. "The same model, make, and color of truck we know the killer used to transport at least one body was stolen from you right before the women were taken and killed."

"Yes, I swear. I don't know anything about the women."

"Why didn't you report it?" Kelsey asked. "You had your truck stolen but didn't report it to the police. You didn't want it to be found?"

"Maybe I will take that lawyer," Randy said. "You can arrest me if you want, but I'm not talking to either of you again until I've spoken to a lawyer first."

CHAPTER TWENTY TWO

John and Kelsey led a handcuffed Randy into the sheriff's office. The office was a hive of activity, and some of the officers looked up, but most didn't concern themselves with the scene. It wasn't unusual to see Randy Frogg brought in handcuffed. The most they got was a slight inclination of the head from one of the younger officers sitting at the closest desk.

Sheriff Anderson came out of his office to greet them.

"What did he do this time?" the sheriff asked.

"So far, he's impeding a murder investigation and wants to talk to a lawyer. Besides that, he didn't get a chance to do anything before Special Agent Hawk took him down in Reggie's." That caught the office's attention; almost everyone looked over eagerly to hear what had happened.

"She got in a lucky shot," Randy said as if he were having a regular conversation and wasn't suspected of murder.

"You don't get to speak," John warned. "You'll get your lawyer, and then you can talk." John led him off toward one of the cells.

"Where are we at?" Sheriff Anderson asked, directing his question at the deputy.

"I don't know. Randy is guilty of something, but I still don't think he's the killer. He's suspicious as hell now that he wants to speak to a lawyer, and John is convinced he had something to do with it. We might know more once his lawyer gets here."

"I'll make sure that happens as quickly as possible. What else do you need?"

Again, it surprised Kelsey how helpful everyone was in the town. It was refreshing, even if Kelsey was still slightly suspicious of it.

"I'd like to look at everything you have on Randy. I want to know him better before I return to question him."

"I'll get that to you as quickly as possible too. How about everything else?" Sheriff Anderson asked.

"We're going to catch him," Kelsey promised.

The sheriff gestured toward his office. She followed him when he walked toward it.

"I'm not going to get in your way," Sheriff Anderson said once they were alone. "You catch this guy, and we're good." He looked down, a little ashamed. "Heck, I don't mean it like that at all. Just keep doing a good job; we're good."

"Listen, I know it's a big change when someone new comes in, but I'm not out to do anything here except my job."

"They spoke about getting rid of me last year. I just thought…."

"You don't need to share this, but if I can get out of this place, I'll leap at the chance. I don't want your job," Kelsey said.

"Give us a chance, and you might like it. At least pretend to like it around here; if you do, people might be a little warmer toward you."

"Goodness knows we could do with the warmth," Kelsey noted.

The sheriff smiled genuinely for the first time since she had met him.

"How are you settling in here? Do you have everything you need?" the sheriff asked.

Kelsey became more guarded when someone was nice to her, and she had to remind herself that they were on the same team. He was not her boss either, even if he felt like one, and he was not out to get her. He had no reason to come after her.

Not yet, but give it time. I seem to give everyone a reason to want to come after me.

"I don't know if I need anything yet," Kelsey added after some thought. "I haven't spent any time at the apartment or in the town. I've been on the case since I got here, and when I'm after someone, I don't have time for anything else. It's cold; that's all I can tell you."

"Yeah, well, you'll get used to that, and it'll still constantly surprise you. Always carry a flask of hot chocolate; that's my secret," the sheriff said, motioning toward the flask on his desk. He patted his belly. "Although, that doesn't help in every area."

Kelsey laughed. It was different from everything she had known. People here were genuine and nice and simple. Not simple in a bad way; they just lived life at a slower pace. She didn't know if she could ever live life at a slower pace, but something about the sheriff made her want to.

"I will get a flask as soon as possible," Kelsey said with a smile.

That seemed to satisfy the sheriff as if he had a goal to have everyone on the team carry around a flask of hot chocolate.

"Take whatever desk you want out there, and I'll have someone get the files out to you. In the meantime, there's coffee in the small kitchen, but you'll have to help yourself to that. I have a feeling we are all in for a late night tonight and every night until we catch this guy."

Kelsey nodded and left the office. She was on her way to the kitchen when a young officer approached. He walked with her to the kitchen.

"Um, Special Agent Hawk, it's a pleasure to meet you and have you on the team. I mean, not on the team, but here to help... here to take the lead on this case."

"Coffee?" Kelsey asked.

The young man looked fresh out of school. Through the door behind, she could see the volunteer deputies who had been called in to help with the case. They were eager to get the job done but did not have the same look as a full-time cop. They weren't jaded or affected in any way. They could go home at the end of the day and forget all about this.

"Um, no. I mean, yes," the young officer said. "Marcy asked me to look into some things for you. I got off the phone with Special Agent Wood earlier in Bismarck. He said he checked out the coffee place, but there was not much he could do without a picture of the suspect, and the staff told him that almost half the guys who come in are creepy. She also asked me to look into any power outages across the state in the past few months. I've emailed you a map of the outages, but I don't know if there's much there. I mean, there have been a lot of outages with the storms, so it might narrow down whatever you are looking for, but it covers a lot of the local area, even on the nights leading up to the murder."

"Every little bit helps," Kelsey said. She added some cream to her coffee and walked back out of the small kitchen with the young officer following her.

"If there is anything else I can help with, please let me know," he said.

"Thank you," Kelsey said. "Will you look into Frank Cobb for me? He was at the hospital with pneumonia. Can you find out how he is doing and if he is home yet?"

"Yeah, for sure," the officer said. "I'll do it right now."

"Thank you, and good work on the case so far."

The officer's face lit up, and it felt good for Kelsey to elicit that response in someone. Perhaps it felt good to be as far removed from her old boss as possible—she could still feel how he had sometimes made her feel. She often projected that onto others, but that was not how things were done here.

Kelsey was returning to her desk when she caught Marcy waving at her. She went to the reception desk instead.

"Sheriff Anderson said to give these to you," Marcy said. "It's all the files we have on Randy Frogg." The pile was sizable. "Hey, did you really take Randy down with one punch?"

Kelsey smiled. "It was more of a chop than a punch." Kelsey mimed doing it for Marcy. "I can teach you how to do it when we get a bit more time if you want."

Marcy's eyes lit up. "Oh, yeah, for sure."

Kelsey nodded and took the files back to one of the empty desks. She could get used to the whole make others feel good stuff. She sat down with her coffee and flipped through the files. She was sure there wouldn't be any previous convictions for murder or abduction, but she needed to get into his head before she confronted him again.

"Is that why?" she whispered when she was halfway through skimming the files. She moved quicker through the second half, following the same thread.

She got up from the desk and went back to the cells. All were empty except for one. Randy sat on the small bed chained to the wall in the only occupied cell, and John sat glaring at Randy from the other side of the bars.

"Randy, what drugs were in your truck when it was stolen? Were you doing a deal at the bar? Is that it?"

Randy looked exceptionally nervous now. "I... is my lawyer here yet?"

"Cut the crap, Randy. I don't care about the drugs, only the truck. Could it have been whoever you were doing the deal with?"

Randy stood up from the bed and moved to the bars. Kelsey approached him but kept her distance so he could not reach out and grab her.

"I couldn't file a report, could I? What if they found the truck with the drugs in it? Then I'm going to jail. We went to look for them instead, but I can tell you one thing; it wasn't the guys we were selling to. Don't ask me how I know; just know that I do. We looked around and asked about the truck, but it just disappeared. Whoever took it better hope we don't ever catch him. There's a target on their back."

"Randy, promise me one thing. When you get out of here, if you ever find the guy, you get your justice, but I want him, okay? This is not a case of making him disappear or anything like that. This guy might have killed three women, and he will kill more if we don't stop him. If you find him before I do, do the right thing, Randy."

Randy didn't say anything, but he nodded. It was the most honest he had been since they had found him in the bar. Kelsey nodded back.

"I need to talk to you in private," Kelsey told John. "I know what I want to do is a bad idea, but I want to make sure there's no other option. And don't try to talk me out of it."

"As if I could," John replied.

CHAPTER TWENTY THREE

The large door slid open, and the man led Rebecca inside—she was still shivering after the incident on the way, and he hoped he wouldn't have to punish her again. He pushed her farther into the darkness and looked out toward the river. This place had never been home for him, but he found something that drew him in. He pulled the large door shut and locked it. Only then did he switch on the small generator. It hummed to life, and the lights did too, illuminating the large work shed.

The man took a cursory look around to ensure everything was as he had left it. No one could get in without breaking in, but he had mice invade his space once. It was winter now, and they would be hibernating—it was only at the start of spring or the end of fall when he needed to worry about pests. There was also the generator failure a few weeks ago, but the low hum sounded as expected. That had annoyed him to no end, but he had put his meditation into practice and regained control so he could see his task through to the end.

He had done well and was happy to congratulate himself on that occasion. He was looking forward to the feelings that would overwhelm him with this one.

When he was happy that everything was in its place, he turned his attention back to the terrified woman in the middle of the room. Her eyes scanned the room: a table set for two, the bed, the large freezer by the wall, a small winch and chains, hooks, tools, a large metal table, and an entire wall of doored shelving units.

He wanted to assure her that he didn't have any plans to have her in his bed, but she didn't deserve an explanation when she did not trust him. She had not yet seen the large cage behind her—a cage big enough for the largest dog or a small woman.

"I am going to take off the zip ties from your wrists and remove the gag from your mouth. Please nod if you understand me."

Rebecca nodded.

"I am treating you respectfully, and I expect you to do the same for me. Please do not scream out—no one is around to hear you anyway. Do you understand?"

Rebecca nodded again.

The man smiled. He removed his knife from his pocket and flicked the blade with his thumb. Rebecca jerked back when she saw it. After all the assurances he had given her, he was frustrated at her lack of trust, but she would soon be free of her preconceptions about people.

He cut the bonds on her wrist and pulled the gag down to her neck. The moment he did, she started to scream.

"HELP! HELP ME! HELP, PLEASE, DEAR GOD, SOMEONE HELP ME!"

The man gave her one good slap across her cheek with the back of his hand to shut her up. So many women and so much disappointment.

"You promised not to—"

Rebecca ran for the door and grasped at the lock, fumbling the large padlock in her cold hands. She pounded on the metal with balled fists.

"What are you doing?" He was exasperated at such behavior. Why did they not want to make it easy on themselves?

He had treated her well and warned her what not to do, but she had gone ahead and done it anyway. She was a guest in his space and had insulted him with her behavior. It broke his heart to do it, but he had to. He went to the tap on the concrete wall and turned it on. He took the hose and uncoiled it from the hooks on the wall. He pointed it at her and pressed the trigger.

The hose was connected to a pump that brought the water up from a well deep underground. It was below the frost line, and while it was cold, it was not as cold as he would have liked. It was hard to keep it cold without accidentally freezing it or setting up a system where his generator ran constantly. That frustrated him, too—he had to work within the confines life had given him.

Rebecca screamed when the cold water hit her, but she lost her voice to the cold soon after. She tried to get out of the stream, but there was no letting up. Eventually, she collapsed in a huddle on the floor as the man hosed her down just as his grandmother had done to him. It had worked in the past, and it worked now. When he turned off the water, she was silent—she was peaceful.

"You know I had to do that," he said. "Now, we can start again if you like, or I can hose you down again. I don't enjoy doing this, but if you continue to disobey me, I will have to."

100

His grandmother had taken no pleasure in it either.

Rebecca looked up at him like a wounded animal. Her lips were blue, but that was her fault.

"I believe you are ready now," he said. "Do you see the partial wall over there?" He pointed to the far corner. "If you go behind, you will find towels and clothes. Dry yourself and come out when you are ready. I know what you are thinking, and I don't want to have to hurt you, so as long as you do as I say, we will have no problems. I have been nothing if not a man of my word. Go and get changed, and if you do not come back out, I shall have to hose you down again. If that does not work, I will be forced to take action you won't like."

The man took the hose back to the wall and wound it around the hook, letting the nozzle drip to the drain below.

"Go on," he said as he turned the water off.

Rebecca got up from the floor by the door and went over to the partially hidden room, her eyes on him the entire time. She disappeared from view. It was solid concrete back there—there was no chance of escape.

The man went to work. He checked the generator to ensure it was still running smoothly—he would need it for the freezing unit when the time came. He boiled some water in a pot over the single propane stove and then made two cups of herbal tea. He placed them on the table and added two plates with bread, meat, cheese, tomatoes, and pickles. He sat down and started to eat.

Ten minutes later, Rebecca emerged shivering from the small room. She looked mostly dry and had chosen black pants and a brown sweater. It was fine, but he would have to redress her in something a little more elegant before she was frozen.

He gestured toward the chair on the other side of the table. "Help yourself, and don't worry, they are not poisoned or drugged. I am not a coward. You will be fully conscious when you face me at the end."

"Please don't kill me," she begged as she sat opposite him, her hands covering her mouth.

"I'm not going to kill you—I'm setting you free. You should thank me."

"Please," she begged again. "I'll do anything."

"Hmm," he smiled. "I think we both know that is not true if your behavior so far is anything to go by. No, this is what you deserve, and I must be the one to do it. I take no joy in it, you must believe me, but I must do it. This is my calling. Please, eat."

Rebecca did as she was told, perhaps hoping her compliance would help somehow.

The man's face brightened. "I have found the perfect place."

Rebecca did not look up at him, but her hand froze midway to her mouth. She did not share his excitement.

"You will be the best one yet. The winter festivals were fine, and we will not talk of the lake, but they were too obvious—too cliché. It will be here, and they won't know how close they are to me—the Midnight Bridge. It is the most beautiful of them all—a beautiful bridge for a beautiful woman."

Rebecca chewed on her bread slowly. Her eyes scanned the table, but there were no knives or forks.

"I paid you a compliment, Rebecca. The least you can do is thank me. I called you beautiful."

"Thank you," she uttered.

This was good—her spirit was broken, her ego removed. She was almost ready for her final form.

"You will cross over, literally, and figuratively. Do you see? The bridge?"

Rebecca nodded.

"You don't," the man complained. "Don't worry; no one can see what I see. Now, eat up, and you will go into the cage."

Rebecca's eyes widened, and she looked around, spotting the cage for the first time. She started to cry, but she did not try to run.

"I need to return to the city, and I shall be gone for two days. I know it is a long time, but it is unavoidable. Not to worry; when I return, I will remove everything from you that is not pure. They will find you on the bridge, and you will be the most beautiful you have ever been."

CHAPTER TWENTY FOUR

"Okay, let me ask you one question. If I go back to Reggie's and talk with the owner," Kelsey started.

"Which is Ernest," John said.

"Of course, it is. Why would this be in any way easy? So, if I go back and talk with Ernest, what are the chances of him letting me take a look at the security footage from when Randy's truck was stolen."

"*If* it was stolen," John said.

"Yeah, I'm with you on that possibility. We need the footage, but how long for us to get a warrant."

"It's already in process, but we won't have it until at least tomorrow. For any other place, I would go in and talk with the owner, but this is a different kettle of fish. We were mostly polite and didn't intentionally insult Ernest, but you took down one of his men, and if you attack one of them, you attack them all. They also won't like us having him here until they know what is happening. I know what you are thinking, but we can't go in there and demand to see the footage without arresting them all. Ernest will give us the footage but on his own time."

Kelsey nodded. "Yeah, I figured as much. I have some stuff to review before we decide on our next move. Do we know when the lawyer will be here?"

"Soon, I've been told. Then we'll have to wait while they talk in private first, then we get to talk with him."

"I have all I need for now. Can you take care of the interview, and we can check in later?" Kelsey asked.

"Sure. I'm not letting him out of my sight until I talk with him. I know you don't think he did it, but—"

Kelsey raised her hands. "We don't work well together if we only think the same way. I hate to be wrong, but I have been. We're not discounting your theory until we can disprove it. If you talk to him, and he confesses, I'll be the first to shake your hand. We cover all the bases."

"All right," John said.

He returned to his post by the cell, and Kelsey returned to the desk. She opened the email on her phone with the power outages in the area and the dates of the outages. The young officer was right—there was no way to search all the locations—and she wasn't completely sure if the killer going to Absolute Zero was because of a power outage. Still, they had to cover all their bases.

Three hours later, Kelsey was no closer to having any information pointing her in any direction. They needed to track the white truck, but Randy and his biker buddies had tried to find it and couldn't. She looked up when John emerged from the back rooms. He came straight to her desk.

"I need to talk to some other people to confirm his alibis for the times of the murders," John said. "I don't trust him, but it all checks out. If his alibis are backed up, he's not our guy, and there might be a killer driving around in a truck full of drugs."

Kelsey sighed. She had been hoping the deputy was right and they could put all of this to rest. "Again, I hope they don't."

"I have a feeling you are right again on this one. I'll call you if I find anything."

"I'll do the same," Kelsey replied.

That all depended on what she found.

It was late when she left the office. The sheriff had gone home hours ago, and another woman at the reception desk had replaced Marcy. A couple of officers were in the break room, but the place had pretty much shut down now that it was past midnight. John had sent her a text saying he had spoken to a couple of people and would check in with the others in the morning. Kelsey said goodnight to the officer at the desk, but she had no intention of going home.

She was headed straight for Reggie's. She was on her own again, but she needed to be at times like this. John would not let her break into the place, and she didn't want to run it by Sheriff Anderson before breaking into a building to recover CCTV footage that might be the key to breaking the case. She could do things by the book, and it might yield the same results, but time was of the essence. They might still catch the guy, but at what cost?

Another dead body?

She could hear the clock ticking in her mind, and it would not stop now. She could feel the killer's haste. He needed to kill again to take control, and he would want to display it somewhere for them after the debacle at the lake. He wouldn't risk a winter festival again, but what did that leave? It would be somewhere public—somewhere it would be discovered and on show. It would be in or around a small town.

Kelsey parked a little way up the road from Reggie's and turned off the engine, cutting her headlights. There were a couple of bikes still outside, but it was almost empty. She waited forty minutes until the last of the bikers left, and then she waited another forty-five minutes until two people came out and locked the door behind them. One left on a bike, and the other left in a car. She gave it a further thirty minutes just to be sure.

After her restless night, and this cutting into her sleeping time, she would be tired tomorrow. She glanced at her watch; it was already tomorrow. Besides, she would not be able to sleep tonight with the adrenaline pumping through her. It was not just the fact that she was doing something illegal, but it was what might happen to her if she got caught. Once she entered the building, the rules changed.

Finally, she got out of the car and made her way over to the building under the cover of darkness. Without the large glowing neon sign out front, the parking lot was pitch black. She didn't want to go in through the front, so she made her way around to the rear of the building, checking for any cars left in the parking lot. There were none. There were no windows on the ground floor, but there were basement windows near the ground at the back of the place.

Kelsey checked around for anyone who might see her—the building obscured the view from the road—and she pulled the small crowbar from her jacket. She had used it many times before and was sure it would be as useful in small towns as in the big city.

She had named it *The Dubious Warrant.*

It got her into buildings, but not often legally. The basement window was pried open easily, and Kelsey slipped inside into more darkness. She had no idea where she was going or if there was anything to find. She had no idea if there was anyone still in the place.

She had watched them leave. Like most times in her life, she was all alone in this. She did not want the sheriff to find out for fear of disappointing him. It was the complete opposite of how she thought about her former SAC at the FBI. She didn't fear disappointing him— she knew he would be disappointed in her no matter what she did. It made her want to disappoint him more.

It doesn't matter if I disappoint the sheriff; he's not my boss. Maybe I just don't want to cause him any trouble.

She couldn't hang around thinking about what she was doing when she was the type of person who usually acted on instinct. Her eyes became accustomed to the dusty darkness, and she chose one of the directions. They both led to more darkness, but one had a better feel.

Kelsey pinned herself to the wall. There was no nightlight, unlike in her dream, but there was a noise. She was sure there was a noise from upstairs. Her breathing slowed until it stopped, and she listened intently. There was only the hum of the building as it rested for the night.

She fought against the fear inside and continued. She would usually not have such thoughts swirling around inside with a simple building entry, but with the dream coming so recently, she was primed with emotion.

She found the room quicker than she expected. The building was not massive, but it was still a welcome surprise when she turned the corner and saw a room with dim light spilling out. She crept closer and listened for another sound—from inside the room and the bar. All sounds had been sucked out of the air. She moved as she had been trained and stayed pinned to the wall until she got to the open door. She quickly glanced in before going back to the wall. The room was empty. She slipped into the room as easily as she had slipped through the window.

A monitor atop an old wooden desk showed the darkness of the main bar illuminated by a single neon sign behind the bar area. She watched the screen for any movement. Then, she found the controls and flicked between the cameras. When she was sure no one else was in the bar, she finally sat in the faded and frayed office chair.

"Don't you move now," the voice from behind said. "You'll regret it if you do."

CHAPTER TWENTY FIVE

Kelsey froze. She didn't turn around, but she could feel the presence of a gun. She had been trained in situations when a shooter had a gun pointed at her back, but that was only used in a standing position, and even then, it was dangerous. She would have no time to get up from the chair and disarm him before he got off a shot.

"Ernest, it's good to see you again," Kelsey said.

"I wish I could see the same." His voice was gravelly, and there was a slight slur; he had been drinking since she first met him that afternoon.

That only made things worse. An angry man with a gun was one thing, but a drunk, angry man with a gun was another entirely.

"I needed to see your security footage," Kelsey said.

"And you didn't think of coming to ask me?" Ernest asked.

Kelsey searched the screen in front, hoping to find something. She found only the dim interior of the bar. The desk in front was no help either—no magic wand that would get her out of this situation. Even if there were a weapon on the desk, she would not have time to reach for it. The only wand she had was the small crowbar in the inside pocket of her jacket, and there wasn't anything magic about it.

Still, she was not afraid anymore. If Ernest wanted her dead, he would have killed her by now.

You're not stupid, are you, Ernest? You know you can't kill me, so how will you turn this to your advantage?

"I would have come to talk with you, but we both know how that would have gone. Would you have let me see the footage if I asked?" Kelsey raised her hands in surrender and slowly spun on the chair to face him.

He had been large in the bar upstairs, but he looked even larger in the dim doorway of the office, lit from the front by the monitor now behind Kelsey. His eyes were a little glassy, and he held a small pistol pointed at Kelsey's chest. She was worried he would shoot her by mistake.

"No, probably not," Ernest said. "That's not the point, though. The point is you broke into my bar, and it's ironic, considering I'm the one supposed to be the criminal, and you are the one who enforces the law. I'd be well in my rights to make a citizen's arrest."

"You would be, but you're not going to, are you?"

"Have you arrested Randy?" Ernest asked. "I want to know how much trouble he's in."

"If my hunch is correct, he should be released tomorrow morning once Deputy Gallant has checked up on a few things. He could have come nicely, but he chose not to help."

"He's an asshole, but he's loyal."

"He also lost a truck full of drugs, didn't he? You never found the truck, right?"

Ernest wavered at the door for a moment. He didn't like that she knew this information.

Kelsey slowly put her hands down and looked him in the eye. "Listen, I'm offering you the same deal. I don't care what any of you have been up to unless one of you is a murderer, but I'm reasonably confident that is not the case, even if Randy threatened to kill me and you are pointing a gun at me. I want to catch a killer, and the footage on your cameras might help. You let me see it, and I leave here without looking into the drugs Randy was selling."

"The drugs are long gone, so that doesn't do anything for me. What do you have to offer in return for the footage?"

Kelsey tried to keep her cool, but she was sick of people messing around and everything slowing to a snail's pace while he was out there, ready to kill again.

"I think he's close to a fourth," Kelsey said. "Even you must care about that. Three women dead, and a fourth coming, and he'll kill again and again until I catch him. If the footage can help, you'll be stopping a killer. Randy is an asshole, but you don't need to be."

Ernest's expression didn't change. He was thinking about it.

"I am an asshole, but not a complete asshole. We look at the footage together, but you owe me a favor."

"A favor? What does that mean?" Kelsey asked. She was ready to agree instantly but didn't want to appear too eager or give him the upper hand.

"Nothing illegal, but you'll owe me," Ernest replied.

"All right," Kelsey said. "Nothing illegal, and if it is not on par with you showing me the footage, I give you a straight refusal, so choose your favor wisely."

"It's a deal," Ernest said, lowering in the gun. He reached around and tucked it into the back of his pants. "Let me in there."

Kelsey got up from the chair, and Ernest sank into it. He tapped on the keyboard much quicker than expected from a drunk biker bar owner, and he opened the menu to search for recordings by day.

"Still remember it," Ernest said. "Was not long after the new year, so most were still off work. We rode up and down all the main highways and secondary roads, searching the towns, but figured someone took it over state lines to sell. Those trucks are worth good money. Didn't think we'd ever see it again. Here it is."

Ernest pressed the button to forward through the footage quickly. The front of the truck was visible parked behind the building, matching exactly what they were looking for: the same make, model, and color. Ernest hit a button to play the recording in real-time.

It hit her like a slap across the face. He had been in town. He probably scoped out the town when he was here to steal the truck.

"There," Kelsey said, pointing at the screen. "That's the guy we're looking for."

"The killer?" Ernest asked.

"It's him. We have him caught on camera in other footage—not enough to ID him positively, but the shoes are the same. He came here to take the truck, and then he came back in the truck to dump the body at the winter festival a couple of weeks later. He doesn't know that we know he is driving this truck or stole it in the first place. Run it back again. I want to check everything."

This could be good. He's out there driving a white truck, but he won't be hiding. He thinks he's blending in, and he is, but we're getting closer.

"Wait, go back again," Kelsey said. "Did you see that?"

CHAPTER TWENTY SIX

"What is it?" Ernest asked.

"There! Stop," Kelsey ordered. She placed her finger on the screen. "Look, you can just about see the tires at the top of the screen. What time is this?" She looked at the timestamp in the corner. "Midnight, right? At midnight, someone arrives in a car at a biker bar and look at the shoes."

Ernest forwarded through the footage slowly until a shoe became visible.

"There!" Kelsey repeated. "That's the same guy. He arrives in the car, and if you forward slowly through the footage again... he disappears from view for about thirty seconds, and then... there! He gets into the truck. He spends enough time at the door that he must be picking the lock, and then a minute later, he backs away in the truck. We only ever see the shoes."

"Yeah, the same guy, but what does it mean? He arrives in one car and leaves in the truck," Ernest said.

"This guy is meticulous—he plans it all out," Kelsey said as if Ernest was her new partner in this case. "Forward through the footage again. I want to see what happens to the car."

They both waited and watched the small sliver at the top of the screen where the car wheels were only just visible.

"There," Kelsey said right as Ernest stopped the footage once more. "Three a.m.; that's when the car drives off."

He wound it back a little, and they both leaned in to see better.

"Someone wearing boots," Kelsey said.

"It could be the killer. Maybe he changed his shoes."

Kelsey shook her head. "No, he wouldn't have wanted to return once he had taken the truck."

"Maybe he had someone come back for the car," Ernest suggested.

Kelsey shook her head again. "No, he would have had the person come with him and drop him off. Besides, this guy will work alone. I doubt he has any friends anyway. He left the vehicle there on purpose. He wanted it to be taken and would have made it very easy to take.

Maybe the keys were left in the ignition, and then when customers leave the bar after a night of drinking, it's there for the taking."

"Are you insinuating that one of us would have stolen a car just because it was there?" Ernest asked.

Kelsey looked to the side at Ernest.

"All right, you make a good point. I'll talk to some of the guys and see what they know."

"Thank you," Kelsey said. "I'd like to send someone down to get a copy of the tapes, but I don't think I'm going to get much else from them."

Ernest nodded. He sighed—he looked tired. "I can let you out the front if you like."

"That's probably the best option," Kelsey said.

She followed Ernest up through the bar, still marveling at how big he was. She could handle herself in a fight, but something told her he would be a tougher match than Randy. The bar was eerily silent as they walked through it.

I don't know if I want to imagine what goes on here at night.

Perhaps it was the small town, but even the criminals were more agreeable than in the big city. She was thankful for Ernest's help and hoped she didn't have a run-in with him in the future. She was not afraid of what might happen; she just liked him.

"Just one more thing," she said when she got to the door. "Why is it called Reggie's and not *Ernest's*?"

"Well, it just sounds better. No one wants to go to a biker bar named *Ernest's*."

Kelsey cocked her head and could agree with that. She left the bar and heard it lock behind her. She wouldn't call her and Ernest friends, but perhaps they were allies. She had seen how the deputy worked, and he did a good job because he knew the people there. She had to assume she was stuck here for a while, and if that was the case, then she had better make the most of it.

Kelsey got back into her car and placed the crowbar under the passenger seat. She started the ignition and drove back to the sheriff's office. Had he driven those same roads after stealing the truck? Had people watched the truck go by and not known a killer was inside? Had anyone driven by him when he had a large block of ice in the bed in the back?

Kelsey could get into his head, but it didn't mean she understood him any better. She understood how childhood trauma or events in a person's life could influence them and make them feel a certain way, even do things. But to kill someone! That was the part she couldn't get her head around. She had read about it in books countless times, but she couldn't fathom how a mind could make those internal connections and turn someone into a monster. In theory, it was sound, but in practice, it felt impossible.

Impossible or not, I need to catch him.

The ticking clock in her mind was getting louder. Every minute she wasted chasing leads was another minute for him to take another woman; if he had her already, it was another minute toward her death. It had not felt like this after the second body or even right after the third, but some force was invading her thoughts. It had always been a race to find him, but now it felt like a race to save his next victim, and it didn't feel like a race they could win.

"He's not stupid," Kelsey said, thinking out loud about the killer. "He arrived at the bar in one vehicle and left in another. He wouldn't leave his own vehicle there, so it had to be stolen. He knew he could steal the truck because he had leverage—he knew about Randy, but he was not close to him. He knows how to find out information. He took the truck and used it in the same place to dump the body. Then he used it to dump two more bodies. He stole it from Winchburgh, meaning he doesn't live near here. He wouldn't steal from his own backyard—that would be too reckless. He might become reckless now, but not when he was planning this out. No, the truck was from here, but the car... the car could have come from closer to where he lives. He steals it near his home and dumps it far from his home, knowing it will be picked up and moved on—it disappears, and even if there is evidence of him stealing the car, it's so far removed that we can't connect it. Where are you? Bismarck? Was that your coffee card we found under the ice, or is that a red herring?"

The adrenaline pumped through her veins as she worked through everything they had. They were inching closer but far too slowly. They wouldn't find him by finding the truck—the search net would have to be too wide—but if they found the first car he stole, they might get something. He wouldn't expect that either. He didn't know they knew about the truck. And he didn't know they knew about a second stolen car—the one he had stolen first.

It gave Kelsey some comfort. Even if they were not getting closer in real life, she was getting closer to solving this all in her mind.

She enjoyed working with Deputy Gallant, but she always did her best work when she was alone. It was when she could think most clearly. She knew that was connected to her past, her childhood, but she didn't want to explore that right now or at all. There was no point in dwelling in the past when there was a future dead body to come.

Kelsey parked back up at the police station. She was unsure what she would tell John in the morning about how she got the footage. She would think of something. Kelsey entered the sheriff's office to the surprise of the woman at the desk, but the woman still gave a warm greeting. Kelsey greeted her in return and then went to the sheriff's office to grab the metal thermos of hot chocolate that was thankfully still on his desk.

She needed to warm up after being out in the snow, and she needed to make a bigger impact on Randy than she had made on the night receptionist. She opened the small plastic cap and took a mouthful. It was not so much hot chocolate as it was warm chocolate—the sugar helped more than the temperature of the drink.

When she reached the jail cell in the back, she clattered the metal flask against the bars, running it the full length. Randy jumped up from the bed almost immediately, though he was still groggy with sleep. He rubbed his eyes and looked over at Kelsey with resentment.

"On the night your truck was stolen, did someone from the bar steal a car from the same parking lot?" Kelsey asked.

Randy looked at her, but he knew better than to try and spin a story or hide information from her.

"I don't know," he said. "But if someone did steal a car from the parking lot, I can almost guarantee who it was."

CHAPTER TWENTY SEVEN

"Arthur Benyon," Kelsey said.

"Yeah, I know him," John replied.

"We know the killer was at the bar, and he took Randy's truck from there. He must have known about the drugs, and I don't know how, but I have the young officer working that angle. The one who looks fresh out of school."

"Peter Johnson," John said with a smile. "Yeah, he's young, but he's eager."

"I can deal with youth," Kelsey replied. "And I love eagerness. I also love that he takes on anything I throw at him, and he does so without questioning me. He might be the perfect police officer."

"He's a good lad—Sheriff Anderson's cousin's son. There wasn't any favoritism, but there are also not dozens of kids lining up to join the sheriff's office in Winchburgh either. Most youngsters are lining up to get out of town and head to the southern states. Anyway, he's a good guy. So, he's looking at the drugs angle?"

"I still think the killer knew about the drugs in the truck, and that could mean he's dealt with drugs before, or he knows the people in this town, or he's been sniffing around. Someone might have heard something. I also don't think the killer is from around here. My gut tells me Bismarck, but I don't have anything to confirm that yet, and there's no evidence to connect him there except for the coffee card, which might not even be his. The white truck is something of a dead end. We know he is driving one, but we can't follow up on every sighting of a white Ford truck, and I don't want to put the word out there yet. If the killer knows we know about the truck, he'll switch vehicles. We can put more patrols on the roads and stop any white Ford trucks on the off chance, but it's like your barn-haystack-needle analogy. Anything suspicious with a white truck—driving in the middle of nowhere, speeding tickets, parked outside places for too long, we take that more seriously. For now, we pay Arthur Benyon a visit."

"If Arthur stole the car, I would be very surprised if he still has it," John said.

Kelsey feared that would be the case. Having the actual car would be great, but a description of it might be just as helpful. They might find DNA evidence in the car, but it would be no good if they had nothing to compare it to.

She was glad John was driving her around again. The roads had been cleared the previous night, but they were still slippery. She still wasn't used to driving around these parts.

"Randy is going to be pissed that he has to wait around for us to do this before I conform his alibis," John said.

"Randy and I had a good chat last night."

John threw her some side-eye.

"He let fly with lots of expletives, but I gave him some in return, so I feel it was very productive."

John shook his head as he turned off the main street and down a side street leading to a residential area.

"How did you *really* get the footage?" John asked.

"I already told you." Kelsey looked out the window at the passing mounds of blackened snow from the plows that had run down the roads a few days ago.

"That's the story you are sticking with? You went down there and asked Ernest if you could take a look?"

"Yeah, completely. What do you think I did?" Kelsey asked.

"I don't know if I want to know. We won't have any trouble with him, will we?"

"No," Kelsey replied.

But he might ask for my help at some point in the future.

"This is the place." John pulled up at the curb outside an unassuming house. "How do you want to do this?"

"Quickly," Kelsey said.

They exited the truck and walked up the path to the door. A garage with the door open was attached to the side of the house, and two large bikes sat inside as if they were on show for passersby. John knocked on the door.

"I hope he's awake," he said.

A scrawny middle-aged man answered the door soon after.

"Arthur Benyon?" Kelsey asked.

"Yeah, who wants to know?" Arthur's voice was weak and hoarse.

"Special Agent Kelsey Hawk," Kelsey said, flashing her badge. "I'm sure you already know Deputy Gallant."

"I didn't do anything," Arthur claimed. "Do you have a warrant?"

"We don't need to come inside," Kelsey said. "If you like, I can take you down to the sheriff's office and toss you in a cell with Randy Frogg, but I don't think either of us wants that."

"Yeah? What's Randy in for?"

"For impeding a murder investigation."

"What? What did he do?"

"He didn't help us; that's what he did," John replied.

Kelsey looked around, but there was no car parked out front. "We are interested in the car you stole from the parking lot at Reggie's, and Ernest is very interested in finding it, too."

That made Arthur uncomfortable. "I don't know anything about any car."

"All right, cuff him, Deputy. Randy will make him talk before he's released," Kelsey said.

"No, wait! What if I did know something? Maybe I saw something, or...."

"Same deal as all the rest," Kelsey replied. "I don't care that you stole the car; I only care about tracing it. Help us, and we have no reason to take you in, Arthur."

He thought about it again and looked up and down the street. It was bad business to have an FBI agent and the Sheriff's Deputy at his door for so long.

"It wasn't really stealing. The keys were in the ignition, and the door was unlocked. We were the last out of the bar that night, and when I saw it there, I knew no one was coming back for it. We all had our bikes, and no one was on the street. It was kinda like a gift, you know?"

"I don't, but go on," Kelsey said.

"I waited until everyone else had left, and then I went back for it. Drove it home and parked it in my garage."

"And this was the same night Randy had his truck stolen?" Kelsey asked.

"Yeah, the same night, but what does that matter? It was like one vehicle was taken, and another was given."

"You didn't think it odd?" John asked. "Maybe it was a gift for Randy."

"Come on, man! I have a family to feed too."

"So, you steal cars to pay for groceries," John noted.

Kelsey placed her hand on John's arm before turning her attention back to Arthur. "Do you still have the car?"

"No. I sold it like a week later."

"I need to know who you sold it to."

'I'll be honest with you; it went to a guy who takes them down to the border. It'll be in Mexico by now, and it'll be long gone."

Kelsey sighed. "What kind of car was it? Do you remember the make and model?"

"Yeah, it was a gray Honda CR-V. It was an easy sell." Arthur almost sounded boastful.

"Deputy, get more information from him. I will call Marcy and get the ball rolling on this." Kelsey turned around and walked back toward the space at the front of the yard, where there would usually be a gate. She pulled out her phone and dialed the sheriff's office.

"Hello."

"Hey, Marcy. I need you to run something for me. Access the NCIC database and find out if there has been a gray Honda CR-V stolen anywhere in the state in the last three months. If there's anything from late December to early January of this year, that's what I'm looking for. If not, go further back and check the surrounding states, too. Call me as soon as you get anything."

"You got it," Marcy replied.

John joined her at the front of the yard as Kelsey hung up.

"Anything?" Kelsey asked.

"Not much more than what he gave you. He claims there was a funky smell in the car, but you believe the car was stolen, right? The killer wouldn't have left...?"

"No," Kelsey replied. "He wants us to see what he's done. He wouldn't have left a body in the trunk."

John beeped the truck to unlock the doors. "I won't tell Arthur that just yet—make him sweat a little. He will come in later today and give a formal statement with everything he remembers. I have a feeling he wants to speak to his contact first—the guy who smuggles the cars down."

"We could bring all these guys in and charge them with what they've told us," Kelsey noted.

"We could, but we won't," John said as they returned to the sheriff's office. "We're only as good as our word, and if we break it, they will never trust us again. If we catch them doing something serious, we bring them in, but if we bring them in when they have helped us, all hell will break loose. This is not a big city. Arresting a gang somewhere like Chicago or Boston is a drop in the ocean. Out here, those guys are the only trouble we have, and they limit the kind of trouble we don't need. There's a time to be cautious."

"Yeah, I know," Kelsey replied. *And I owe Ernest.*

Kelsey's phone rang.

"Marcy?" she asked.

"One hit in the last three months for that make and model—and you were right about the timing. January 4th in Bismarck. I'm downloading the file now, and I'll send it over to you."

"Marcy, you are a star," Kelsey said before she hung up again.

"Good news?" John asked.

"I'm going to Bismarck. Can you drop me at my vehicle?"

"No," John replied. "We go together. Besides, you can't handle these roads yet."

CHAPTER TWENTY EIGHT

"We are going to be on my home turf now," Kelsey said.

The town was far, far behind them, and they were back on double-lane highways. She had been a little nervous driving around in town, even being driven around, but the roads were wide again, and they were so well used that there was no layer of snow with tracks to drive in. It felt wonderful to be driving on asphalt again.

"You didn't grow up in Bismarck, did you?" John asked.

"No, far from it, but it's a big city. You know the small-town folk, but the city is a different animal."

"We'll see. I have visited the city, you know. I've been to Europe too, backpacking as a young man. I bet I know the cities a lot better than you know the small towns."

"I know the people," Kelsey said, trying to gain the upper hand.

"People are not so different. When I was backpacking through Berlin, I met a bunch of folks. Small towns, big cities, rural, urban; we're not all that different. People are people."

"People are people?" Kelsey laughed. "That's how you are going to finish the story? It all sounded so deep until then, and you finished with people are people."

John laughed, too. There was no reason to be happy when the killer was still out there, but Kelsey at least felt she was doing something about it. They were on the move, physically chasing the trail, and while the ticking clock was getting louder and louder, she was starting to feel that it was a countdown to facing him.

They had packed quickly, John saying goodbye to his family before they left for Bismarck. The other officers would chase up everything else, but Kelsey could feel they were heading in the right direction. The coffee card and the stolen car all pointed to him living in Bismarck. He lived in the big city but killed in the small towns.

"He grew up in a small town," Kelsey said.

"What's that?" John asked as he took a bite of his granola bar.

"I'm just thinking out loud. Whoever this guy is, I would bet on him growing up in a small town; that's where his trauma happened. He goes back to small towns to kill and display, and it helps him to control it."

"I still don't understand any of this. Does it help us to catch him?" John asked.

"I don't know. It's helped in the past. The more you know about someone, the easier it is to determine what they might do. People are people, right?"

John laughed. "People are people."

Kelsey knew they shouldn't be laughing about this, but just as the killer had to kill to manage his trauma, they had to laugh to control their feelings. If they gave in to what they were chasing, they could go to very dark places.

"How is your family doing through this?" Kelsey asked. "I know it can be hard when working cases like this. Back in Valleyview, almost no one at the FBI had a family, and those who did, didn't maintain them all that well."

"I'm not going to lie; it's been hard over the past few weeks, but my wife understands why I have to put in the hours. My wife and daughter are scared, too. I know he takes single women, but what if he adapts? I can't live with my wife and kid while there's someone out there like that."

"Yeah, I want to get him too."

But for very different reasons.

Kelsey took out her phone and looked through the file again. "Tall, likely black hair, and larger than average, Caucasian is our best guess with the grainy footage, and dressed in black slacks and a black jacket. Nothing flashy about him, nothing distinctive, but he is a big guy, so he is a man who might be noticed. He wore black to steal the car, but he's a performer too—he likes to put on a show—and he might dress more outlandish or colorfully when going about his day-to-day business."

"It's not a lot to go on," John sighed.

"It's not," Kelsey admitted, "but it's more than we had. Each connection we make gives us a little more information about this guy, and that brings us closer to him. Yesterday, we didn't know at all what he looked like, and now we have a decent outline. We follow the process, and we will eventually find him."

"What happens then?" John asked.

"He won't want to be caught. I've read about killers like this and caught some. This whole thing is a performance; he would rather go out in a blaze of glory than be locked up and forgotten. We win if he dies at the end of this, but we win more if we can take him alive."

"What if he takes you with him?"

"You don't need to worry about me," Kelsey replied.

"I do worry about you," John replied.

"You might have been responsible for soldiers in the past, but you are not responsible for me."

She knew that putting herself in more danger was a distinct possibility. There was no doubt she would put herself in danger to take this guy down. They drove quickly and quietly toward Bismarck. The radio was turned down low, the faint hum of Country and Western music playing.

When they reached the city, they went straight to Cappa's Coffee Place. Special Agent Wood had already spoken to them but didn't have a description when he went. They parked a block down the street in the first parking spot and walked to the coffee shop.

"Good afternoon, and welcome to Cappa's."

"We need to speak to your manager," Kelsey said.

"Oh," said the teenager. "I hope, um—"

"Don't worry, we're police. No one is in trouble; we are just following a lead and hope we can get some information." Kelsey flashed her badge, speaking quietly so as not to disturb any customers. She had already checked out the place to see if anyone was matching the vague description in the place.

"Yeah, yeah. Brian!"

The teen stood with pursed lips, nodding to himself until a middle-aged man came around from the back. He raised his eyebrows in greeting. Kelsey flashed him the badge and explained why they were there.

"I don't know if I can help you, but I will ask the staff. We get a lot of people coming through here each day," Brian said.

"Any CCTV?" John asked.

Brian shook his head. "We don't get any trouble, and there's nothing to take. I know I should probably get some, but it's expensive. Sorry, I'm going on. Oscar! Coffee for these two, full discount." Brian gestured toward Kelsey and John. "Do you want to take a seat in the café, and I'll see if anyone can be of any help."

Kelsey looked around the café one more time, but no men matched the description in the police report. Kelsey didn't believe in the supernatural but could sense him as if he had left a trail for her. She didn't know where it led, but she sensed his presence—his evil.

They took a seat at the back of the large open seating area, gaining a view of the front door, and were brought a couple of coffees a minute later.

"What do you think?" John asked.

"I don't know. I think we're on the right track, but I don't know how. I feel like he's going to walk through the door any minute. If we wait long enough, he will come to us."

"Looks like someone else is coming to us." John gestured over toward the young woman with a name tag approaching them.

"Um, hi," she said when she got to the table. She lowered her voice. "I'm Maria. I, um, think I might know the man you are looking for."

CHAPTER TWENTY NINE

"Just take it nice and slow, Maria," Kelsey said.

Maria sat at the table with them and looked nervous. She looked around from time to time as if he might be watching her.

She took a deep breath. "His name is Grant. That's the name he always gives us to put on his cup, but I don't know. There's something weird about him. I don't think that's his real name."

"That's okay; you are doing great, Maria," Kelsey soothed. "Grant, he's a white male?"

"Yes."

"And he's tall, right? Big and tall?"

"Yeah, he's a really big guy." Maria looked around the café again as if her life might be in danger.

"And black hair?" Kelsey asked.

"Yeah, black hair."

"Great; that's great, Maria. Now, when you heard that description from your boss, what stood out? Why do you think your customer might be the man we are looking for?"

"I don't know. A feeling."

"A feeling?" John asked.

"I know it sounds silly, but you wouldn't be asking about someone if they hadn't done something bad, right? You are both cops." Maria wrung her hands together as she spoke.

"Has he done something?" Kelsey asked, worried that he had hurt Maria.

"No, nothing that I know about, but he's just really creepy. I know that sounds silly too, but I get like this really, really bad vibe from him."

"I get that from people, too," Kelsey admitted. "It's good to trust your instincts, Maria. Is there anything he has done to make you feel this way?"

Kelsey continued to scan the coffee shop in case he walked in.

"It's the way he looks at me. He's old, like Brian. Like, not old-old, but a lot older than me, but when he looks at me, it's like he's thinking about doing stuff with me. It makes me feel icky just to serve him. And when I hand him his cup sometimes, he makes sure he touches my hand. And he always mentions something about how I look, and it might be a compliment from anyone else, but when he says it, it's like he's expecting something in return, or that he's doing you a favor. I don't know what it is, but he gives off serial killer vibes, you know."

Kelsey nodded. "I know what you mean, Maria. All of this is very helpful. Can you tell us anything else about him? Eye color? Facial markings? Does he have a beard? A tattoo? How does he dress?"

"I try not to look him in the eye, so I'm not sure, and he doesn't have any scars or a beard or anything. He's like colorful—he always wears bright colors; like not all over, but a bright scarf or tie or something. And when he's not talking to just me, it's like he's an actor or something, but a really bad one who thinks they are good but are not, and no one has told them. Sorry, I'm not making much sense with all of this."

"How about his shoes? Have you ever seen him wearing shoes like this?" John asked, taking out the eBay listing he had printed off.

Maria shook her head. "I don't know. I'm usually behind the counter, so I don't notice his shoes. I know I'm not being much help."

"Maria, you are really helping us," Kelsey said. "We know a lot more about him than we did before. And how regularly does he come into Cappa's?"

"Every few days, but I haven't seen him in a while. What did he do?" Maria asked. "Should I be worried?"

"No, you shouldn't be worried. We don't know that he has done anything until we have spoken to him, so don't worry, all right? Just go about your day as you normally would, and know that we are here if anything happens." Kelsey tapped her pen against the table. "If you feel unsafe, find someone to walk you home, or we can have someone walk you home, but that's only if you want it. There really is nothing to worry about."

"Okay, yeah, maybe," Maria said. "Um, Brian said I can get you some more coffee and food if you like. If we are done, that is."

"We are all done," Kelsey said chirpily. "And more coffee sounds great. We haven't had lunch, so we will gladly eat. Thank you, Maria."

"Thanks, Maria," John added.

Kelsey waited until Maria was gone before she said to John, "Can you get on the phone and see if there are any cops who can come down here at closing to walk people home? I don't want to worry anyone just yet, but I want to make sure Maria is protected. If he has taken a liking to her, she might be his next victim. She fits the profile, as far as I know."

"I'll get on it," John said.

He went outside to make the phone calls, and while he was out, Maria came over with some more coffee for them. Kelsey smiled and tried to look as chipper as possible to put her mind at ease. She would talk to the manager later, but she and John would have to stake the place out until the suspect came back. She felt helpless again, having to wait, but she felt close enough to reach out and touch him. She sipped from the mug and had to admit that it was damn fine coffee.

John returned after making some calls. "Okay, I told them not to send any uniformed officers here in case they spook the guy. They are going to send someone down here later to liaise with us, and Special Agent Wood is going to call you sometime today to offer any help he can. What are you thinking? We wait here and hope to catch him?"

"That's the plan. We leave at closing, get a room somewhere, and come back again tomorrow."

"You do remember I'm married, don't you?" John quipped.

"Don't worry, I'm not that type of person. I can't think of anything worse than doing that to someone." Kelsey had tried to forget what had happened in Valleyview, but it had traveled there with her.

"I believe you," John said. After a couple of seconds, he added, "You don't need to tell me, but it's all connected, isn't it? How you are, the way you are driven, getting in his head. I can see the pain in your face at work every day. I don't want to pry into your life, but if you want to talk about it, I'm here for you. It does help, you know."

Kelsey sighed again. "Yeah, I know."

She had been to many therapists, and none of them had helped her—not the ones she visited as a child, nor the ones she had tried as an adult. Therapy wouldn't help. Only justice would set her free—justice or revenge.

"I grew up in Missouri," Kelsey said. "Born and raised in a small town about the size of Winchburgh. I couldn't wait to get out, and I did. Moved to the big city and lived the dream as an FBI agent."

"And now you are right back where you started," John said.

"Yeah, I am. And the man who put me here is not happy with just that, from what I've heard. He's pissed that I came here willingly or as willingly as I could pretend I was, and he is even more pissed that I have a big case to work on. He will be even more pissed when I catch this guy."

"He sounds like an asshole."

"He is." Kelsey smiled.

"Sheriff Anderson once shouted at me for taking two donuts when he didn't get any, so I know exactly how you feel."

Kelsey laughed and almost spat out her coffee. "Should we get the manager to give us some donuts to take back when we are done here?"

"We talked it out, man to man; almost came to a fistfight, but we are good now," John said. "Seriously, though—if I didn't have enough motivation to catch this guy, you just gave me some more. We take this guy down, and then we rub your old boss's nose in it. We're supposed to be a team, but there are still guys like that around. Hey, maybe it's a blessing that you got out of all that and came here."

"Maybe." Kelsey was starting to think that maybe that was the truth. The big cities were where the crime was, and she was damn good at catching bad guys, but if she could do the same up here in North Dakota, she could still prove herself.

But to who? Who am I trying to prove myself to?

That was another question with no answer. Herself? Her parents? Her boss? The world? Maybe it was all of them. She looked out the window, hoping to spot a large man with a colorful scarf. He lived and walked among them, and no one knew. Maria might suspect something, but she didn't truly know the monster he was. He was a regular guy to most people, but to three women, he was the last person they saw. He would be the same for a fourth.

Kelsey didn't know if he had taken four women so far, but she consoled herself with the fact that it wouldn't be Maria. If he came in regularly, he might have formed an attachment, making her a target in the future.

"It was a home invasion," Kelsey said quietly.

John turned to face her again, and he gave her the time to speak.

"When I was ten, my mother, father, and sister were killed in a home invasion. They were murdered in their beds, but I was left. I hid in a closet until the police arrived and I was discovered. They never found who did it. I don't know why they were killed or by whom, but whoever came into my house that night did so with the intent to kill. They didn't take anything or do anything other than kill. I think that's why—"

Kelsey froze. She knew as soon as he entered the coffee shop that he was their guy. He fit the description exactly, and he wore a pair of bright purple gloves. Kelsey only had to see the look in his eyes to know. He had an aura about him, and she could feel the evil radiating from him from across the room. She looked at John quickly, and he had spotted the man too.

He wore an easy smile and looked immediately at Maria when he walked in, smiling wider and heading for her at the counter. Maria tried to act normal, she really did, but she could not help glancing toward the back of the room and catching Kelsey's eyes. There was a look of understanding, an acknowledgment that they were dealing with something far worse than she suspected.

He saw where she was looking and couldn't help but look too. He glared at Kelsey and John as they stood, and the smile left his face. They were not wearing police uniforms, but the man knew they were there for him.

Time slowed down. Kelsey thought about going for her gun, but civilians were all around. She didn't have proof that he was their guy, but the look on his face told her everything. She wished at that moment when time stood still that she could shoot him in the chest, but she couldn't—she might break the rules to catch criminals, but only when she could put herself in danger, not others.

The man took a breath and turned toward the door. Time sped up as he slammed into the person behind him, knocking them to the ground. A scream erupted as a woman was also knocked over. Kelsey sprang into action first, followed by John. They tore out of the coffee shop after him.

Kelsey was not going to let him slip through her fingers.

CHAPTER THIRTY

When she exited Cappa's, she was surprised to see how much distance the suspect had put between them—he threw pedestrians to the ground, but Kelsey didn't have time to stop and help them. She didn't know if John was right behind her, but she trusted he was and pushed as hard as she could, pounding her feet into the sidewalk and dodging left and right as pedestrians stopped and stared—becoming obstacles.

The man rounded the corner without looking back. Kelsey rounded the corner soon after, and while he hadn't put more distance between them, she had not caught up either. He was a large man, but he was fit. Kelsey would chase him to the ends of the earth. She still didn't look behind to see if the deputy was with her; she didn't want to lose sight of him.

He wasn't running for his car. He was either ditching it, or he didn't have a car with him. Kelsey hoped it was the latter; that meant he lived or worked close. When faced with danger, people always ran toward safety. This guy was intelligent and meticulous—Kelsey hoped he had the same instincts as everyone else. She needed to stay close enough to see him enter his safe space.

The suspect ducked suddenly into a nondescript apartment building. *Yes, yes, yes!*

He wouldn't have entered the building unless there was something for him there. Either he was fleeing toward something, or there was something where he was headed that he didn't want anyone to see. Kelsey could only dream it was someone he had taken.

She didn't see which way he had gone, but there was only one way to go: up. Kelsey took the stairs two at a time unit she got to the third floor. The door to the hallway clicked shut. She was about to reach for it, but it didn't feel right. She froze and listened.

No one is that gentle when they are being chased.

A second later, the door to the floor above slammed shut. She raced up the stairs again and burst out into the hallway. No one was there, but she heard an apartment door click shut up ahead.

Kelsey raced for the apartment—she was sure the deputy was not behind her anymore. She pulled her gun without thinking. Her old SAC would relish the chat he would have with her for pulling her gun in a building without knowing what lay ahead and without waiting for backup, but she wouldn't have cared. She would have used the gun if he was still her boss and only hoped Sheriff Anderson would understand. And whoever else she pissed off in Bismarck by doing this.

She pointed her gun at the lock and fired. There was no way she could break through the door with her shoulder. She fired five times into the lock and then kicked the door open, aiming the gun into the apartment. No one fired back at her. Another noise from far inside. It wasn't a scream or a sound of surprise—this was the right apartment. She moved through, checking the room to her left to clear it. She moved past the bathroom, catching her reflection in the mirror.

She saw the back of him as he climbed out the window.

"Freeze!" she shouted.

He did not freeze and disappeared from view before she could fire a warning shot. She ran to the window, gun pointed. When she reached it, a large boot slammed into her arms and chest, knocking the gun from her grip. She struggled to get up—the sound of boots on metal receded quickly. She finally pulled herself up to the window and looked out.

He was gone.

"What the hell!" John shouted from the doorway. "I only knew you were up here because of—"

"We don't have time!" Kelsey shouted. "I don't know where he went, but he's going to her. He's desperate, and he needs to finish what he started. He has her somewhere, and we need to find her soon because he will kill her if we don't."

"What do you need?"

Kelsey looked around the living room and kitchen—it was a mess, but an organized mess. There were stacks of books, papers, files, pictures, maps, and dozens of other items.

"It's here somewhere," Kelsey said. "Get his description out to as many cops as possible, and I want his description released on as much media as possible. He knows we are after him now, and he will act hastily. Get that done, and come back and help me search this place."

John nodded as he pulled out his phone and moved toward the bedroom to make phone calls, scanning the place.

Kelsey didn't care about preserving evidence—she needed to know his next move. She flipped through books and files, photographs, and maps. The large map on the wall showed Bismarck and the larger surrounding area. There were dozens of small towns on it. Kelsey looked closer, hoping to find markings, but it was clean.

She pulled out her phone and pulled up the list of places where there were power outages in the days leading up to the first murder. She looked around the large desk below the map and found some pins. She pushed one into each small town on the map with a power outage. That only narrowed it down to eight places—they were all possibilities.

"John!" she called.

He appeared on the phone a moment later. He was talking to someone, and she hoped he could multitask. She pointed to the map.

"We need people in each of these towns looking for a white Ford truck. If it's not on the road, it'll likely be by a large warehouse or storage unit."

John nodded and approached the map. He looked the map up and down as he spoke on the phone. Kelsey looked at the map once more before returning to the desk in front of it. She sat down in the leather office chair and stared at the map. She imagined the killer sitting in the same chair, looking at the same map, and planning where he would take the women and where he would kill them. Winchburgh was on the map, but it didn't have a pin in it—it was not where he had killed the first victim, only where he had displayed her.

She returned her attention to the table in front, picking up documents, files, books—so many books—going through them as hastily as possible for some clue to his whereabouts. One of the books was a diary, which led to the discovery of multiple diaries. She flicked through them quickly to find scribbled notes and sketches, but there were no dates. It was a treasure trove for behavioral scientists but not for someone who needed the information immediately. There was no book with blank pages.

Did you take the most recent one with you? Is that what you came back for?

Some themes flowed through the diaries—water, cold, mentions of his grandmother—but nothing was coherent; nothing pointed to a place. There were no names of people or places.

I could be who I was meant to be.
But they cannot.
The journey will take them there.
I am Charon.

The short handwritten verse chilled Kelsey, the cold from the book seeping out and getting under her skin. There were numerous short poems interspersed with the more mundane musings and sketches.

They pass from this life to the next.

But not without my hand.

I am the bringer of life.

She didn't want to read his thoughts, but they were the key. He was not feeding her information, but they were clues to the bigger picture. They were his real thoughts; his intentions were there if only she could find them.

"What do you have?" John asked, coming off the phone briefly.

"I don't know. It's here, but I can't find it."

"We'll find him," John soothed. "A team will be here soon, and they can go—"

"Shut up!" Kelsey shouted. She did not mean to be so brash, but there was no time for politeness. "Just give me a moment."

She looked at the pins in the map, the files, documents, books, scribbles, and receipts. It was a giant puzzle where no pieces fit. She opened the diary she had picked up previously and flicked back to a page.

She gave me the cold to teach me. I resented her, but hate was not enough for her. The cold washed away my outer shell, and I could finally see. Hate and love are so intertwined.

She held it open and grabbed another diary.

I take away their shell.

But rise above.

I guide them over.

With hate and love.

"I know where he has her," Kelsey said.

CHAPTER THIRTY ONE

"You're sure about this," John said as he drove.

They didn't have a siren or lights to attach to the top of the truck and could only hope they would not be pulled over. They could talk themselves out of it, but it would slow them down and waste precious seconds. The killer was on his way to her, and he would act quickly once he got there.

"I am," Kelsey replied.

She was not completely sure, but it all made sense. It had to be where he was going.

"I did suggest you visit the City of Bridges, but not like this," John said. "You really think he'll try and put this victim on one of the bridges?"

"I think that was his plan. I don't know what he will do now, but it won't be anything good. He's not going to let her go, and he won't go down without a fight."

John pulled his truck into the other lane without indicating and passed a brown SUV. "And you got all of this from the diaries?"

"The diaries, the map, the power outages. That's why he went to Absolute Zero to free her. The power outage knocked out his equipment, so he had to improvise."

Kelsey sounded sure as she spoke, but she still doubted herself. Even as she explained it, there was no concrete evidence that he was headed for the City of Bridges. All she had were some loose clues and a gut feeling.

"The pins in the map were the locations of the outages. His base of operations is in one of the towns. After the lake, he needs something big. He needs to complete what he started. I'll be honest with you; I don't think he planned for it to be like this. I don't know if he consciously chose the City of Bridges or if it was a subconscious attachment. I've been skimming through his diaries. They are all over the place but form a rough picture of his life and thoughts. His grandmother did something to him when he was young. Maybe made him take ice baths or tried to drown him; I don't know. There was something with cold water. That's why he freezes them. It's his form of control over his past trauma. He wants to rise above it. That's what drew him to the bridges. It's all connected. He takes them over the River Styx just like the boatman Charon. He guides them into the next world. He is the bridge. And now, he will use the bridges for his last display. It wasn't planned as his last, but he knows it will be. This part of the process has always been inside, waiting to break out. I don't know if he understands his own thoughts, but..."

"You do," John finished.

Kelsey thought about it. What did it make her that she could understand all of this? There was a fine line when it came to a case like this. To catch a killer, you had to think like a killer.

"I can see it from the outside in. He uses the diaries to get the thoughts out but doesn't interpret them. They influence him, and he wants that, but he doesn't see how hurt and damaged he is. He has taken control, but not in the right way. It is all laid out in the books."

John was silent for a while before he said, "I don't know if I ever want to understand this stuff. Don't get me wrong, I'm glad you do, but I'm not strong enough to understand it all. It would mess me up."

I'm not strong; I'm desperate. I just need to work out where that desperation is taking me.

"It would mess anyone up," Kelsey said uncomfortably.

"I know it would," John said quietly.

Kelsey had been through the worst trauma imaginable and needed to find control in her life, just like the killer. So far, she had channeled it into her work, but with every risk came the possibility of slipping into madness.

The town came into view, and it looked beautiful. The road was elevated and led down into a valley. From the highest point, eight of the bridges could be seen as the river snaked through the town. Buildings were collected on either side of the river, with large homes dotting farmland around that. As with every town Kelsey had visited since coming to North Dakota, it was covered in a blanket of white—the river included.

Kelsey leaned forward, looking at each visible bridge in turn—each one a different shape and color—to spot a block of ice.

Please don't kill her, you bastard! Use her as leverage, and we can take you both from this town alive.

"It's, um, beautiful at night when the bridges are lit up," John noted.

Kelsey could hear the nervousness in his voice, but she didn't doubt it would look beautiful—a wonderland hiding an atrocity.

"He won't be in the center of town. Look for any large buildings on the outskirts," Kelsey ordered.

They slowed to the speed limit as they entered the town limits. Red barns dotted the square fields outside the main residential area. He wouldn't hide her there. Not secure enough, and he'd have the possibility of other farmers visiting. It needed to be unwelcoming but still blend in.

"There!" Kelsey called. The nerves were contagious and took root in Kelsey's stomach when she spotted it.

John slowed and looked to where she pointed, checking for the next turnoff, but he didn't see what she saw.

"The tarp! White like the snow and covering a vehicle," Kelsey said.

John nodded. He turned off onto a minor road leading to the row of warehouse units. He didn't want to drive too quickly and alert him to their presence. He stopped the truck beside the tarped vehicle. Kelsey leaped out first, drawing her gun. The road was quiet behind them. Trees lined the other side of the warehouses, with the frozen river beyond them.

Please still be here.

Kelsey pointed her gun at the large door to the warehouse and moved toward the tarp. She pointed the gun with one hand and bent down to grab the bottom of the tarp with the other. She lifted it up to reveal the side door of a white truck. John looked over and nodded in agreement. Kelsey didn't think he had tried the same move as back at the apartment building. He was in too much of a rush to park outside one building and enter another. He would need the truck again to transport the body. Besides, she could see some discoloration on the outer wall of the concrete structure where water had seeped through and damaged it.

Kelsey nodded toward the padlock on the door. It was open; someone had unlocked it.

"We know you are in there!" John shouted. "We have the building surrounded. Come out with your hands up, or we will be forced to come in!"

There was no answer.

"Come out with your hands above your head!" John tried.

Kelsey shook her head.

John inched toward the door. Kelsey pointed her gun at the large slab of metal and held her breath. John gently took the handle, and in one swift motion, he slid the large door open. The darkness engulfed them.

It was not only the darkness but the noise. A loud hum complemented the darkness—a generator. The sound of splashing water came from the back of the building as if someone was thrashing around in a bath.

And then came water—biting cold water rushing at them like an arrow. Kelsey lifted one hand to shield her eyes and thought about firing toward the source, but she couldn't risk hitting the victim. She could risk a lot, but not that.

"We have you—" John started.

The water stopped, replaced instantly by a large figure bundling toward them, and neither had time to react. Kelsey shivered as the water froze to her skin in the biting cold. A flash of metal, cold as ice, slashed through the air, cutting John across his chest. He spun and fell to the ground, blood flowing from under him. The figure smacked into Kelsey before she could get off a shot. She spun too and fell to face John, quickly rolling onto her other side, still holding her gun. She aimed it toward the back of the running man as he left the warehouse and headed for the tree line. Her vision was blurred, and her arms shook from the force of his hit and the water.

She fired until the gun was empty.

CHAPTER THIRTY TWO

The killer continued to run and disappeared into the trees. Kelsey leaped to her feet, but her attention was split. The killer was getting away, but the cause of the splashing was apparent. Someone was in a large container at the back of the room, and they were submerged.

I need to catch him!

Kelsey was frozen to the spot, literally and figuratively. She was alone again, but there was too much to do by herself. She had to let him go to save the woman drowning. It was the right thing to do, no matter how much it hurt. She moved into the building, but a hand grabbed her shoulder and pulled her back. She turned and raised her fists to fight.

The gun pointed at her stopped her in her tracks.

"Take it," John urged.

She dropped her empty gun and grabbed the deputy's, staring at his bloodstained jacket—the red already turning to ice.

"Don't worry about me. It's just my arm. Go! Get that bastard. I'll get her out," John said.

Kelsey glanced toward the splashing water before she ran from the room and sprinted for the tree line. It was hard going; her clothes were sheets of ice, frozen to her body and slowly freezing her. There were places to hide, but this was not like the city. He could hide for a while, but the town was small, and he wouldn't risk going back for his vehicle. It was only a matter of time. She approached the trees with her gun held in front of her.

The woman in the warehouse was still alive. She trusted John to get her out and stop her from drowning. She would take care of the killer.

Now that she was away from the road, it was deathly silent. The darkness between the trees was oppressive. When she entered the woods, she heard a gentle hum—the sound of water still moving below a seat of ice and a covering of snow. It was faint, but it sucked all other noise from the area. There were no birds chirping, no animals of any kind, no cracking of branches to suggest where he had gone or even if he was still in there. Each step through the ankle-deep snow was like walking through deep sand, and even with the adrenaline pumping through her veins, her body shivered with the piercing cold.

Then, a whoosh through the air.

The branch smacked against her forearms before she could turn and point the gun. A shot was fired before the gun dropped to the snow, but it didn't hit him. Kelsey's instincts kicked in, and she jumped back as the branch came back up, threatening to smash into her chin. She smacked into a tree and rolled to the side, falling face-first into the cold.

There was no time to feel sorry for herself or take a second to recover. Kelsey pushed herself back to her feet and turned to face him just in time to see the flash of metal. Kelsey ducked under the slash and came up behind his arm. She pushed his arm away, and the blade slammed into the trunk with a thud, but he didn't drop the weapon.

Kelsey took her chance and slammed her elbow into his temple. It shook him a little, but it didn't slow him down. The knife came back around, and his eyes were wide and wild. Kelsey could see the future reflected in them: this ended with one of them dead. She moved back and felt the cold tip of the knife brush her cheek.

The killer lunged at her. She did not have the strength to stop him from knocking her down, and he fell on top of her before rolling over her. He was heavy, and he was strong. She was no match for him.

I don't have to stop you; I only have to keep you busy until help arrives.

He grabbed at her ankle, but she managed to kick him away. He was strong, but she was fast and agile. She got to her feet before he could and took a couple of steps back to be out of range. When he stood, he growled at her like a wild animal. He held the knife and started to circle, ready to finish the job.

"Kelsey!" The shout came from nearby.

The killer turned and ran.

"In here!" Kelsey shouted.

She ran after him, not caring about the danger. They would fight again, and he would get the better of her, but it would be worth it. If he escaped her, he would escape the town. She trusted others, but not as much as she trusted herself.

Kelsey burst out of the trees. He was right before her, and he had stopped. No, he hadn't stopped; he was climbing the chain-link fence that separated the woods from the frozen river. She didn't hesitate. She ran to the fence and climbed as he threw himself over the top. It had slowed him down a little. She reached the top and jumped, landing on his shoulders. The momentum took them both forward down the incline toward the river.

She felt her ribs battered as he rolled over her down the snowy hill. She hit her head on something. And then the piercing cold as she smashed through the ice and entered the river. Her body shut down for a moment. She reached up and slammed her fists on the ice above. She was in complete darkness, and death had come for her. It wasn't cold or painful anymore; it was pleasant, and she sunk into it.

You won't ever find their killer!

Kelsey thrashed around in the water, needing to find the way out. If they came through the ice, they could exit through the same hole. There was a light up ahead. There was no way to tell if it led toward life or death, but she swam for it through the numbing cold. She reached the hole but didn't have the strength to pull herself through.

A hand grabbed her jacket, pulling her out of the water and onto the ice. The deputy had made it to them and saved her. She choked back the water and looked up into his eyes. He was angry. It was not the deputy—it was the killer.

Before she could do anything, he wrapped his hands around her neck, choking her. She grabbed his wrists, but he was too strong—an immovable force. She tried to shout obscenities at him, but the words were stuck in her chest. She felt her eyes bulge, and her life slipped away again. She was too numb to feel the full extent of the pain as her airways were closed.

"Why did you do that!" he demanded. "Why did you do that?"

"I… didn't," Kelsey managed.

"I've done my best! I tried my best!" He rocked back and forth as he strangled her. "I don't understand. I gave you death. That was our promise that you wouldn't do that again."

He thinks I'm his grandmother. He killed her, too.

"You faile—" she gurgled.

"I what?" the killer asked, needing to hear from her.

The grip on Kelsey's neck loosened ever so slightly. She looked into his eyes but scanned her periphery for anything.

"You failed me," Kelsey said.

The killer's eyes widened. He was hurt. The grip on her neck loosened enough for her body to stop panicking, even if it was not enough for her to breathe. She let go of his wrists and felt around in the snow. Her hand clenched around a large rock. The killer's expression moved from hurt to anger again, and there was a flinch in his fingers as he tightened his grip. She pulled the rock from the snow and slammed it into the side of his head.

His hands left her. She finally took a long breath in, but she didn't relax. She pushed him off as he slumped to the side, but his movements told her he was not knocked out. She took sharp, painful breaths. She managed to get to her knees at the same time as the killer. She pushed herself to her feet, and he faltered and fell on his back.

Kelsey held the rock tight in her hand. Blood flowed from the killer's temple, and his eyes swum as he tried to focus on her. The knife lying not far from his body caught her eye. She dropped the rock and picked up the knife, holding it as tightly as she could as the strength left her.

She stumbled toward him and collapsed on top of him. Kelsey swung her leg over and straddled his chest. She rose and fell with his stunted breath. She held the cold blade to his neck, knowing he deserved death.

I can't save those who have died, but I will stop you from hurting another soul.

She pressed the blade into his fatty neck tissue until a drop of blood appeared. The tears blurred her vision, and she looked away.

He deserves this! They did not!

Kelsey closed her eyes, the lifting of his chest becoming more even. One swift movement and it would end the pain—just not hers.

She let out a guttural animal moan and slammed the knife's hilt into his temple instead.

CHAPTER THIRTY THREE

Kelsey stood outside the building and took a deep breath. She didn't want to go inside. The door opened as someone exited, and the noise flooded out. The door closed again, leaving her in silence on the street. She could tackle a killer after being plunged into frozen water, but entering this place with the people inside made her want to turn and go back to her small apartment. She wouldn't have to think or talk or any of that other stuff that was expected of her.

Still, she had promised to be there and was a woman of her word.

Kelsey took another deep breath and breached the entrance.

It was loud when she entered Jacob's Tavern. It would typically be busy on a Friday night, but it was tripled with the officers drinking heartily and the additional townsfolk who had come to celebrate. This was not their victory, but the person who had caught the serial killer terrorizing a wide area of North Dakota was one of their own.

Kelsey didn't feel like one of them, but they had accepted her as one.

John waved over from the tables on the other side of the bar, and from the way he was leaning in close to the woman beside him, she assumed it was his wife. Kelsey had not thought about what came after her failed engagement, but she couldn't imagine being in a relationship right now. She shouldn't have been in one in the first place—her ex might be a dick to do what he did, but it hadn't been fair for her to believe she was committed to him. She was too messed up to be with someone who couldn't understand her.

The deputy left the table and came over to greet her. Possibly because Kelsey had not moved from inside the entranceway since she entered the bar.

"You going to come join us?" John asked. "My wife is dying to meet you. I think you might be her hero."

"Yeah, I'm coming over—I just needed a moment. Have you heard anything yet?"

"Nothing concrete, but the doctors are sure Rebecca Jones is going to make a full recovery. They are treating her for hypothermia, but her other injuries are all superficial—most of them from when she was stuck in the tank."

"Thank you for getting her out," Kelsey said.

"You don't need to thank me; it's my job."

"No, I know."

She was thankful, though. All of this would have meant nothing if they had gotten there only to have her die.

"And Richard?" Kelsey asked.

"He denies everything, but he's going to prison. If you ask me, he wants his day in court. He knows he's guilty, and if what you have told me is anything to go by, he wants to be on a stage, right?"

"See, you are as messed up as I am."

John chuckled.

"I can almost guarantee that he will represent himself. He's smart, but he's also insane. It will be his big moment, and he'll take on the challenge of proving his innocence, but if he can't, he'll be happy with the fact that people will know his name. We need to do all we can for people to remember the victims' names and not the killer's."

"You need a drink," John said. "There are about three dozen beers on the table. We've had regulars buying us beers all afternoon, but they're really for you. You do realize we wouldn't have caught him."

"We're a team," Kelsey said.

"We might be, but a team is only as good as their leader. Just don't let Sheriff Anderson hear me saying that. Come on, come, and join the rest of us. We won, and we deserve to celebrate."

Kelsey followed him over to the table, and everyone stood up to greet her. Kelsey feared they would give her a round of applause, but they didn't. A couple of townspeople clapped her on the back as she walked by. It was unsettling, but there was a part of her deep down that liked it.

"Special Agent Kelsey Hawk!" Sheriff Anderson called, raising his bottle of beer.

"Special Agent Kelsey Hawk!"

Kelsey gave a sardonic smile and took the beer she was offered. After it was clinked a dozen times, she took a drink. This was usually the moment when the breath was released, and the tension was washed away, but this wasn't the end for Kelsey. Evil had been taken from the streets, but more was out there.

"Thanks to Kelsey, a life was saved three days ago," Sheriff Anderson announced with a large smile. "We don't know how many others were saved by her actions. Richard Gibson is behind bars where he belongs."

There were loud cheers throughout the bar.

"Three women died," Kelsey said grimly. "We shouldn't forget them." She raised her bottle with a grimaced smile and took a drink.

The others nodded along and took drinks somberly.

The noise died down a little as the officers chatted among themselves. Sheriff Anderson walked away from the group and gestured for Kelsey to follow him.

Here it comes! Time to get chewed out, even though I did my job.

"Three women died," he said, "and nothing will ever bring them back. I know it is hard to celebrate the lives saved when those women died, but it is not about celebrating the win; it is about hope." Sheriff Anderson looked over Kelsey's shoulder toward the table of officers. "We are celebrating, so we can believe it is over. We are marking this day and telling our children they are safe again. When we celebrate together, the young women of our town feel safe again on the streets. This is not about winning or losing; it's about our people and what they need."

Kelsey coughed. "Sorry, I thought you were going to shout at me for a moment there. I'm used to that."

"Oh, I want to, Hawk. I want to because I think it's the only way to get through to you. I don't want them to hear me, so imagine I'm shouting this next part at you." The sheriff's expression turned serious, but his voice remained whispered. "They look to you, Hawk. You got them here, and they will follow your lead tonight, but so help me God if you don't go over there and buy shots for everyone and actually be the leader you are supposed to be. I know I am not your boss, but I am ordering you to have a good time tonight and celebrate this. I am ordering you to have hope!"

Kelsey looked at the sheriff and blinked. His voice was quiet and reserved, but she could see his frustration bubbling behind. She nodded and did exactly as she was told. She went to the bar and ordered a tray of shots, waiting there to take it over herself.

"Hey, you mangy lot are not nearly drunk enough yet," Kelsey said when she returned to the table. "Come on! We saved lives, and it couldn't have been done without all of you working on this. So, stand up, take a shot, get blackout drunk, and dance this night away. Who's with me?"

There was a stunned silence for a moment before everyone stood and cheered. The party had been restarted. Everyone downed a shot, and the volume in the bar rose.

Kelsey still didn't feel like celebrating, but she knew the sheriff was right. She pulled out her phone and re-read the message she had received the day before.

We all get lucky sometimes. Good thing you didn't get anyone killed with your recklessness. Don't worry, I'm waiting for you to mess this up, as always.

She didn't need to trace the anonymous number; she knew it was from SAC Paul Granger. It would be eating him up inside that she had done so well not even a month into her post in North Dakota, and he would still be working behind the scenes to ensure she failed.

Don't worry, boss! Come for me all you want, but I'm not playing nice anymore. I might be reckless, but I get the job done while you sit in your ivory tower.

Kelsey looked around at the mood she had created. Sheriff Anderson patted his deputy on the back. Everyone else was laughing and drinking. She was used to being reamed out for not going by the book—she could get used to being forced to buy her colleagues shots and get them drunk.

Maybe this place is not so bad after all.

EPILOGUE

One Week Later...

Kelsey looked down at the newspaper clipping she had looked at a thousand times before. Each time she read through it, she expected to notice a detail she had not noticed before, such as a mention of how the bodies were positioned or the name of an officer that was odd, but it always read the same. It gave no details other than the fact three people had been killed while sleeping. Kelsey knew more details than anyone else, and she still knew nothing.

No, that's not true. The killer knows more than me. They know everything.

When there was a knock at the door, Kelsey quickly slid the sheet of newspaper back inside the folder and pushed it to the side. Deputy Gallant poked his head around the corner a moment later.

"Hey, I thought I would bring you some coffee. What with you being so busy and all that."

Kelsey smiled. "I love it and hate it at the same time. After the ice-block killer, I'm all done with excitement. Still, being behind this desk all day is killing me."

"What *have* you been up to?" John asked, entering the room, and sitting down on the chair on the opposite side of the desk.

It had been a few days since she had spoken with the deputy or anyone at the sheriff's office.

"Admin work. I never had the chance to do any of that when I got here. I hit the ground running, so to speak. Some professional development, too. The law is always changing, and then the technology we use is always changing, and the law enforcement techniques are always changing." She shook her head and laughed. "A big part of the job is keeping up with the changes. Then there's also the community engagement Sheriff Anderson suggested."

"And?" John sipped his coffee.

"I'm trying to stay as busy as possible so I don't have to go into a school and give a talk or try to talk to people on the street. I know everyone wants to talk to me after what happened, but I'm not much of a people person."

"You do alright," John admitted.

"I'm going to have a lot of time on my hands," Kelsey admitted. "When I was sent here, it was supposed to be like this, but fate and evil had other plans. I don't know what it is about this place, but it gives a fresh perspective. I don't know the perspective, but my mind is not as loud as when I was back in Valleyview. Things are simple here—in a good way."

"Simpler," John sighed. "That's not the word I would use to describe these past few weeks."

"I'm not explaining it very well. I'm talking about this." Kelsey dragged the thin folder to the middle of the desk, turned it around, and opened it.

John scanned the headline, and his face dropped. "Your family?"

Kelsey nodded. She waited as he read through the article. When he was done, he grimaced and closed his eyes tight for a second.

"I'm sorry," he said. "I can't imagine what you have gone through—what you are still going through."

"I thought I could bring them back somehow by catching the worst of the worst, but it doesn't help. It briefly takes my mind off it, and when I'm done, I'm back where I started—nothing has changed. I'm afraid they will be all I can think about if my professional life is like this going forward."

"Speaking from experience, the case you just solved is all the excitement you will have around here."

"I need something to focus on, and it's time to go back to the beginning. They looked into the case, and I know they treated it seriously, but they didn't find any leads worth following. I don't know. Maybe the technology has advanced enough, or it just needs a fresh pair of eyes. Maybe someone needs to look into the case like their life depends on it."

Because my life does depend on it. If I don't get any closure from this case, I'm never going to be free,

"You wouldn't rather see out your time here without doing this? You might not find anything," John asked.

"I know, but I have to try. If I'm going to be sitting on my ass, I might as well put my time to good use."

"All right," John said. "Listen, I have to get to work, but if you need anything, you only have to ask. I know you like to do things alone, but you have the backing of the sheriff's office. Don't tackle this by yourself, okay?"

"I'll try," Kelsey conceded.

John stood up and nodded. He left the office, leaving Kelsey with her thoughts.

A part of her had been dreading looking into the case. It had been investigated twenty years ago, and it remained unsolved. She worried she would end with the same result. Every case she had solved, every criminal she had put behind bars, had done nothing to help her. If she investigated the deaths of her parents and sister and found nothing, she would forever be a failure.

And that failure would be worse than any failure she had experienced before.

But it wouldn't stop her. She had to know.

NOW AVAILABLE!

DEAD RECKONING
(A Kelsey Hawk FBI Suspense Thriller—Book Two)

Tough and brilliant FBI special agent 30-year-old Kelsey Hawk is relocated to the desolate and unforgiving landscape of small town North Dakota, to which she'd vowed to never return, when, in a remote area, a body is found frozen to death. Kelsey, with few clues, suspects foul play—and enters into a deadly game of cat and mouse and soon realizes she may be walking right into a killer's trap…

"This is an excellent book… When you start reading, be sure you don't have to wake up early!"
—Reader review for The Killing Game

DEAD RECKONING is book #2 in a new series by #1 bestselling mystery and suspense author Kate Bold, whose bestseller NOT ME (a free download) has received over 1,500 five star ratings and reviews.

When she was just a child, Kelsey's entire family was murdered, leaving her, the sole survivor, to grow up in the foster system. A rising star in the FBI, Kelsey set her ambitions on being assigned to a field office in the big city, away from the ghosts of her past. But when she's reassigned to a small town in North Dakota, she can't help but remember all the tragedy she fought so hard to leave behind.

Can she stop this killer in time?

A page-turning and harrowing crime thriller featuring a brilliant and tortured FBI agent, the KELSEY HAWK series is a riveting mystery, packed with non-stop action, suspense, twists and turns, revelations, and driven by a breakneck pace that will keep you flipping pages late into the night. Fans of Rachel Caine, Teresa Driscoll, and Robert Dugoni are sure to fall in love.

Future books in the series are now available.

"This book moved very fast and every page was exciting. Plenty of dialogue, you absolutely love the characters, and you were rooting for the good guy throughout the whole story... I look forward to reading the next in the series."
—Reader review for The Killing Game

"Kate did an amazing job on this book and I was hooked from the first chapter!"
—Reader review for The Killing Game

"I really enjoyed this book. The characters were authentic, and I see the bad guys as something we hear about daily on the news... Looking forward to book 2."
—Reader review for The Killing Game

"This was a really good book. The main characters were real, flawed and human. The story went along quickly and wasn't mired in too many unnecessary details. I really enjoyed it."
—Reader review for The Killing Game

"Alexa Chase is headstrong, impatient, but most of all brave with a capital B. She never, repeat never, backs down until the bad guys are put where they belong. Clearly five stars!"
—Reader review for The Killing Game

"Captivating and riveting serial murder with a twist of the macabre... Very well done."
—Reader review for The Killing Game

"WOW what a great read! Talk about a diabolical killer! Really enjoyed this book. Looking forward to reading others by this author as well."
—Reader review for The Killing Game

"Page turner for sure. Great characters and relationships. I got into the middle of this story and couldn't put it down. Looking forward to more from Kate Bold."
—Reader review for The Killing Game

"Hard to put down. It has an excellent plot and has the right amount of suspense. I really enjoyed this book."
—Reader review for The Killing Game

"Extremely well written, and well worth buying and reading. I can't wait to read book two!"
—Reader review for The Killing Game

Kate Bold

Bestselling author Kate Bold is author of the ALEXA CHASE SUSPENSE THRILLER series, comprising six books (and counting); the ASHLEY HOPE SUSPENSE THRILLER series, comprising six books (and counting); the CAMILLE GRACE FBI SUSPENSE THRILLER series, comprising eight books (and counting); the HARLEY COLE FBI SUSPENSE THRILLER series, comprising eleven books (and counting); the KAYLIE BROOKS PSYCHOLOGICAL SUSPENSE THRILLER series, comprising five books (and counting); the EVE HOPE FBI SUSPENSE THRILLER series, comprising seven books (and counting); the DYLAN FIRST FBI SUSPENSE THRILLER series, comprising five books (and counting); the LAUREN LAMB FBI SUSPENSE THRILLER series, comprising five books (and counting); and the KELSEY HAWK MYSTERY series, comprising five books (and counting).

An avid reader and lifelong fan of the mystery and thriller genres, Kate loves to hear from you, so please feel free to visit www.kateboldauthor.com to learn more and stay in touch.

SOMETHING DARK (Book #4)
SOMETHING TO HIDE (Book #5)

Made in the USA
Las Vegas, NV
29 June 2024

91665861R00094